Murder at the People's Theater
An Erica Duncan Mystery

by

Laura Shea

Copyright 2017 by Laura Shea

For information, email **Cozy Cat Press**, cozycatpress@aol.com or visit our website at: www.cozycatpress.com

COZY CAT PRESS

ISBN: 978-1-946063-35-9

Printed in the United States of America

Cover design by Paula Ellenberger
www.paulaellenberger.com

1 2 3 4 5 6 7 8 9 10

Many thanks for the encouragement of my intrepid band of readers: Karen Galatz, Laureen Griffin, my sister Sally Sweeney, and Deborah Williams. Your continued support has made all the difference.

CHAPTER 1

"O brave new world,
That has such people in't."
William Shakespeare, *The Tempest*

"This is the People's Theater. Erica Duncan speaking."

"Good. Now try it again, but this time with more feeling."

Erica looked up from her desk. She didn't have far to look, given that her acting coach and new boss, Dessie Harris, was barely five feet tall in clogs.

"I'm supposed to add drama to the way I answer the phone?" asked Erica.

"This is the People's Theater. We add drama to everything" was Dessie's answer, as she flung out her hand to punctuate her last word.

"You should use that in the next ad campaign," Erica offered.

"It's been done," said Dessie. "It was the fall of 2009. We did a Shakespeare, a Sam Shepard, and a little musical that made us a lot of money."

"Little musical?" Erica raised her eyebrow.

"Yes," Dessie continued rapturously. "We all know that the People's Theater would be a dim memory without *The Brothers Wittgenstein*. Who knew that the tale of a philosopher and his family of geniuses—set to music—would pay our way into the twenty-first century? But people really liked it, and not because the critics told them to."

"As I recall, old Ludwig and the gang were more than a little flaky," said Erica. "If they'd had the pharmaceuticals in those days, the happy-pill truck could have pulled up and parked in front of the Palais Wittgenstein—and they would still have been short on anti-depressants. Besides Baby Ludwig, the philosopher king, there was Rudy and Hans, both of whom committed suicide in their early twenties. Right?"

"Plus brother Karl, who took his life in his forties," added Dessie.

"But my favorite is Paul," sighed Erica.

"Are we talking about the Beatles or the Brothers now?" asked Dessie.

"Both," Erica replied. "But for now, let's stick to the Brothers. Paul, the concert pianist who lost his right arm courtesy of a Russian bullet in 1914. Paul, who spent time in the same Siberian prison that Dostoyevsky made famous. And in spite of it all, Paul kept on playing."

"Are you going to swoon?" Dessie asked.

"No," said Erica, "but you've got to be impressed by a guy who continues his concert career—single-handedly, as it were."

Dessie winced.

"And it was he, not Ludwig," Erica declared, "who was the famous brother, at least during their lifetime. Paul even commissioned one-handed musical compositions—"

"Which he allowed no one but himself to play," finished Dessie.

"Who else could?" asked Erica.

Dessie shrugged. "You really know your *Brothers Wittgenstein*."

"I listened to the cast album until it wore out," Erica said. "I'll never forget the part where Paul plays that one-handed concerto. That was something."

"I love that part too," Dessie replied. "And that other song he does, in the first act, when he's practicing the piano, and he shouts at Ludwig, who's off in another room—"

"'I cannot play when you're in the house!'" quoted Erica.

"'As I feel your skepticism seeping towards me under the door!'" Dessie finished. They both laughed, and Dessie said, "Martin had a shot at that part." Quickly shifting her position, she added, "Well, he auditioned."

"Your husband?" said Erica. "Your late husband? He was an actor."

Dessie nodded, her face speaking volumes about the sadness she still felt.

Erica planned to review Martin McNulty's career with her boyfriend, Alan, who was an actor who'd known Dessie and her husband earlier in their careers. For the moment, she nodded appreciatively and said nothing.

Dessie picked up the conversation. "By the way, saying *that* in front of me is fine. Saying it in front of the boss would be a bad idea."

"Saying what?" asked Erica.

"The part about how the People's Theater wouldn't be here if not for *The Brothers Witt*," Dessie answered. Erica started to respond, but Dessie cut her off.

"We all know it's true, Erica. Just keep it to yourself."

Years of teaching had taught Erica how to read an audience. She might be on a self-imposed exile from the academic life, but she had not lost her touch. New to the People's Theater—today being her first day in their employ—it was already clear to Erica that Dessie Harris was the boss in everything except title and salary, regardless of what the organizational chart might say. With no plans to repeat her comment in front of anyone, Erica chose to praise instead.

"It's perennially listed as one of the greatest musicals of all time," she began. "I mean, the Kemby, and all the other awards it got—"

"Unfortunately, we weren't eligible for a Nobel Prize," said Dessie. "We tried, believe me. I filled out all the paperwork. But the committee wouldn't budge."

"In any case, everyone here must be very proud of *The Bros*," said Erica, "especially the boss."

"I think she hums the overture in her sleep," Dessie replied. "Assuming she does sleep. But to tell you the truth, our single greatest success—at least, of the commercial kind—fell into her lap. She happened to be in the building when the director came knocking on our door, looking for rehearsal space. At the time, it was her job to give him an empty room to work in and to keep an eye on the production. When his little idea turned into a hit musical, *she* turned into a big-time producer, and the People's Theater lived to see another day. Lots of them, in fact."

"Yes," said Erica. "I guess that one hit kept things afloat for you during a few—shall we say—dry spells. Sorry about the mixed metaphor."

"What's a mixed metaphor?" asked Dessie. Without waiting for an answer, she said, "Thank goodness for the show *and* the touring companies *and* the tee shirts *and* the coffee cups."

"Not to mention the key chains," Erica added.

"I love them all," Dessie replied. "They paid our salaries and put people's children through private school. Not my children, of course. But it just goes to show that family dysfunction never goes out of style, especially on an epic scale."

"It had a beat, and you could dance to it," said Erica. "Assuming you could waltz."

"Three suicides in two acts. Not exactly family friendly," said Dessie. "And putting it to music was its own kind of risk. That risk, I think, is what the boss wants to be remembered for."

Erica knew Dessie meant Alexa Wallace, the Producer at the People's Theater, a woman in a role usually performed by a man. That may be why she went by the name of Alex. The success of *The Brothers Wittgenstein* had been quickly followed by the death of her predecessor, a theatrical entrepreneur from the old school, who relied on a ruthless charm—it wasn't only his cigar that smoldered—and a charisma that sometimes smoothed his path and just as often left others churning in his wake. Unfortunately, he succumbed to a variety of health problems to which attention had not been paid for over a decade. In the long run, major organs will not be ignored.

After the roller coaster ride of the previous regime, the theater's board of trustees needed a soft place to land, and Alex, in her sensible pumps and tailored suits, accessorized by expensive scarves and more expensive perfume, seemed just the ticket. With an appearance as buttoned down as she was, Alex, at first, had to work to look older than she was. Now, she didn't have to try. With no known bad habits nor a companion of any kind—not a pet, not even a plant—the pressures of running a theater might have eliminated a personal life if there had been any evidence of one in the first place.

"Based on our short acquaintance, I'd put Alex in the vast expanse of middle age," said Erica. "Somewhere between forty and death."

"Forty-five and counting is more like it. And that 'forty and death' reference didn't get by me, I'll have you know. I did *Mame* in summer stock," Dessie said.

"Recently?" asked Erica, too new to know better.

"Oh, no," said Dessie. "Years and years ago."

"You were . . . ?"

"Mame, of course."

Not my first guess, thought Erica, who said, "My last place of employment was a veritable quote-fest. But I'll try to control myself."

"Yes, Alan said something about that. You were a teacher, weren't you?"

"A professor, actually."

"Remind me why you aren't anymore."

"They were offering me the possibility of lifetime employment."

"And who would want that? I can see why you left."

"It was a little more complicated."

"Isn't it always?"

"And now that it's September," said Dessie, "do you miss being in school?"

"Strangely . . . no," Erica said, as if considering this for the first time.

"Well, I'm just glad I ran into Alan when I did," said Dessie. "We had a need and you filled it. We needed someone to read and edit our publications. You don't have to worry about the plays, or the press releases, for that matter. There are departments that do that. We need someone like you to read other kinds of things, the boss's public statements for one, then fix what needs to be fixed. And now we've got our own Ph.D. to do it. At least while you're between engagements. And believe me, there's no shame in being between engagements."

"No shame felt here," said Erica.

"It's a fact of life in this business," Dessie continued. "And don't worry about the telephone greeting. The only phone you'll be answering is your own. Oh, and one other thing," she quickly added, "your language in the office has to be sodium-free."

"What?" asked Erica.

"No salt. Save the dirty words for later."

"Oh," said Erica, finally understanding. "Not a problem, Dessie. I was a teacher. We cuss at home. Or at least we wait until we're a quarter mile down the drive."

"Okay," said Dessie. Her face reflected an unmistakable confusion at Erica's last remark, but she soldiered on. "Alex wants everyone to sound professional."

"I'm guessing that *professional* is a big thing with Alex," said Erica. "What's with the suits?"

"Well, as you may have noticed, the dress code around here is pretty casual. We don't pay people enough to expect too much in the style department, and it would violate the whole working-class ethic of the People's Theater if anyone got too snazzed up."

"Anyone but Alex," said Erica.

"Once upon a time," Dessie began, "Alex looked like the rest of us and took the tee-shirt-and-jeans route. When they made her the big boss, she started to dress like a committee woman, with the suits and a tasteful hairdo. No one forced her to do it. She just did."

"I'm sure it inspires confidence at board meetings," said Erica. "And the big donors can breathe a sigh of relief, handing over their contributions to someone who looks more like them than—"

"The rest of us?" Dessie interjected.

"Most of us, anyway," finished Erica. "When I think of Alex, it's a clatter of heels and a whiff of perfume as she scuttles by on her way to another important meeting. Of course, that's based on my one meeting the day of my interview."

"Which was only a formality, by the way. Your reputation preceded you."

"Oh?" asked Erica.

"I mean that in a good way," said Dessie, about to make her exit. "Be glad, Erica. You have a great spot, sitting where you are. Just two doors down from the boss. And one door down from me."

"And there actually is a door," said Erica. "For this we are truly grateful. Especially after seeing the cubicle arrangement on the other side of the building."

"Yes, that's where we keep our ambitious youth," said Dessie. "Maybe *cage* is more like it. The People's Army. They're going to change the face of American Theater. Just ask them. And they're always making up excuses to come over to this side of the building to see what's going on. Or more specifically, who's going into Alex's office. Sooner or later, anyone who's anyone walks through that door. And *you* have a ringside seat."

"I *am* a lucky girl," said Erica. "Why didn't you stash me over there with the Theater of Tomorrow?"

"Are you kidding?" said Dessie. "For them, the main topics of conversation are 'what I need, what I want, and what I'm willing to do to get it.' I wanted a grown up to talk to."

"Me too," Erica agreed.

"They'll probably send an emissary to check you out," said Dessie. "You did get an office, a real office, a great office, in fact, so there's the possibility that you can be useful to them. If not, they can still be jealous of you."

"There are gonna be some sad little faces when they find out I'm of no use to anyone, unless spelling and punctuation are an issue," Erica replied.

"It won't be," said Dessie, nonchalantly. "They represent every race, creed, and fancy college known to man or woman. Then throw in a trust fund or two."

"I get the picture," said Erica. "But what happened to the working-class values? The *People's* Theater?"

"They're still in effect. It's just that these folks are among the few who can afford them. You may have noticed that the pay scale—"

"Is on a downward spiral," said Erica. "Yes, I did see that. This theater takes 'non-profit' seriously. Which means they can starve, or Mummy and Daddy can fill in the gaps?"

"Clever girl. I knew you would get it," said Dessie, who made another move to leave the office, then stopped in front of Erica's prized door. "I have a few things to do before the morning is over, but why don't we get lunch later? I can answer all of your questions, especially those you might not want to ask in a semi-public place."

"I'll work on a list," Erica said.

"Dessie?" a new voice asked. The question came with more than a hint of a whine.

"What is it, Claudia?" was Dessie's slightly pained response.

In the doorway of Erica's office stood Dessie's assistant, Claudia Winthrop, who was chewing on a piece of the long brown hair that hung on either side of her face, like curtains that were almost always drawn. "I have a question about this letter?" she asked.

Claudia's tone suggested that she was as unsure about asking the question as she was about the letter.

"I'll be right with you, Claudia," said Dessie, giving her a dismissive look. Erica watched as Claudia turned and walked back to the office she shared with Dessie.

"She's supposed to make my life easier," Dessie confided to Erica. "I don't see how, when she needs an explanation for everything. But she's right beside me, eight hours a day. With an hour off for lunch and good behavior."

"Hers or yours?" Erica asked.

"Depends on the day," replied Dessie.

"I look forward to our lunch," said Erica. "I feel a few questions percolating."

Several hours later, Erica and Dessie sat at an outdoor café across the street from the theater.

"I hope he's a better actor than he is a waiter," said Erica when their salads finally arrived, looking slightly disheveled from the bumpy ride to the table.

"He's fumbled everything up to and including our request for water—tap, not sparkling," Dessie said. "And let's not forget the sugary ice tea. We can leave him to his own unfortunate future."

"And his unsatisfying tip," Erica added.

"So you had questions? Fire away," said Dessie.

"Okay," Erica began. "Starting at the top. Where's the boss today?"

"Taking her one day off a year. Always the same day. September 16. The only day she takes until next year."

"Why? Is it her birthday? Is she having a party?"

"Her birthday's in June. She takes this day every year, and we don't ask why. She'll be back tomorrow, and believe me, she never looks like she's been to a party. "

"Duly noted. Now explain Claudia."

"Honestly, I can't," Dessie answered. "She's been with us for about six months. I'm usually swamped, and I needed someone to pick up the slack. And there she was."

"You didn't go for one of the army of the ambitious?"

"Well, what I like about Claudia is that she's quiet. Strange, but quiet. And she doesn't have a phone. Or if she does, she doesn't bring it to work. Those things drive me crazy. And yes, I have one. I have two kids, so it's a given. And I'm well aware that most of our twentysomethings go through life clutching at least one form of technology. Either their parents handed them a smartphone at birth, or they waited and let them teethe on it. I just hope this particular form of technology doesn't harm their hearing."

"A brain tumor would be more like it," said Erica. "So far, studies have found no harmful effects, but most studies are only a few years old, so they can't really consider long-term use. And the studies don't differentiate between the casual and the heavy user. From what I've read, there are a number of brain surgeons who use the ear piece or stick to the speaker phone."

"Really," said Dessie, impressed. "You *are* going to be a lot of fun to have around. When you do meet these people, I wouldn't start with cell phones and brain tumors. Not the best ice breaker. And the phones don't seem to affect their work. Then again, nothing seems to affect their work. They just keep plugging away. I just didn't want to listen to the constant ringing or buzzing and the whispered conversations that follow. That's why Claudia is sitting where she is."

"Big mistake?" asked Erica.

"Nothing I can't fix," said Dessie. "Claudia's only vice, as far as I know, is a notebook that she scribbles in when she thinks I'm not looking. Not that I care. Scribble away. Just get your work done. And a few less questions wouldn't hurt."

"Hers or mine?"

"Oh, hers," Dessie said, reaching for her glass of iced tea and grimacing after she took a sip. "You can ask away."

"Claudia scribbles in a notebook? How old-fashioned of her," said Erica.

"Old-fashioned, yes," Dessie agreed. "It's even an old-fashioned notebook. One of those black marble composition books. The kind my kids use for copying out their spelling words for the week. As far as

Claudia's concerned, no technology, that's fine with me. But no clue? I object to that."

"I thought you did the hiring, Dessie."

"Usually, I do. But she wrote some heartfelt letter to Alex from her tiny town in who knows where, Maine, I think. Something about her dreams of the bright lights in the big city. Anyway, Alex invited her for an interview and then took her on."

"That was nice of her."

"I think Claudia reminded her of herself, at least from a distance. Up close, not so much. Alex is a small-town girl who had her own dreams of life in the big city."

"Did they come true?"

"Some of them. Not all. They never do," said Dessie, staring wistfully into her salad.

"I guess that's where the resemblance ends," Erica ventured.

"What?" asked Dessie, looking up from her salad.

"Claudia's to Alex," said Erica.

"Oh, Claudia is no Alex," replied Dessie, in an even tone. "When Claudia got the job, she gave Alex this gooey-eyed thank you, which was the last time we saw that expression of gratitude on Claudia's face."

"What did Alex do?" Erica asked.

"Well," said Dessie, "she was polite, for Alex. She mumbled something that sounded vaguely like 'you're welcome.' Then she looked like she had somewhere else to be. And she went there."

"So, Claudia's not a member of the army of the ambitious?" Erica asked.

"Not even a charter member," said Dessie. "The rest of them are wired and ready for action at all times. And speaking of wired, Erica, the coffee in the office is something you might want to avoid. Claudia makes it. Mighty strong stuff. It looks and tastes and sometimes even smells like latex paint. I don't think she's trying to poison us, but that's our Claudia."

"There must be something she does right," said Erica.

"There would have to be," said Dessie. "She can type. In fact, she can type very fast."

"What?" asked Erica, laughing at the robotic way Dessie had delivered her lines.

"I'm quoting from her letter of application," Dessie said.

"So the ability to type very fast put her over the top?" asked Erica.

"Something must have," answered Dessie. "She's here, isn't she? Any other questions?"

"None," said Erica. "I'm out for the moment."

"Then I'll ask," said Dessie. "How's the boyfriend? Or whatever you people are calling each other these days."

"I call him Alan. Sometimes Mr. DeLorme, but only on special occasions. And he's great. He's working on a film."

"How's that going?"

"Well, from what he tells me, it's mostly sit and wait. Then sit and wait. Then sit and wait some more."

"I love it so far," said Dessie.

"Then maybe they get to a scene he's in, then it's more sit and wait. There's a lot of setting up of shots. Alan shows up in a lot of shots, kind of lurking in a corner. He has this great little part, a slightly crazed guy named Ned."

"The screenwriter must have been up all night coming up with that name," said Dessie.

"Well, it works, actually, because the ordinariness of the name sets you up for the weirdness of Ned. This part could really get people's attention. It's going great for him."

"That's a lot of 'greats,'" said Dessie. "Is there a 'not so great' somewhere in there?"

"No, not really," said Erica. "I would never begrudge him his success. I know how long and how hard he's worked for it. Maybe I don't see him quite as much as I would like. With his filming schedule, it's kind of hit or miss. For the last few years, when we lived in different places, I didn't see a lot of him, but *that* I could understand. Now I *live* with him, but our hours don't always coincide."

"But you do run into him. That would be enough for some people," said Dessie with a wry smile. "It also sounds like a temporary condition. I mean, filming will end sooner or later."

"That's true," said Erica, wishing she hadn't brought it up.

"Where have they been filming?" Dessie asked.

"Oh, all over the city," Erica replied, relieved by the quick change of topic. "I went to watch one day. To me, it looked like a giant tangle of cable wire and people. They were filming a street scene, with loads of extras. There was this one guy," Erica remembered. "His entire role was to walk to the corner and come back. Walk to the corner and come back. So he would walk to the corner and come back until they called 'cut.' Then he did endless head rolls while shaking out the tension in his hands and arms. It was walk to the corner and come back, but you would have thought that the emotional weight of the film was on his shoulders."

"An actor prepares," said Dessie.

"This guy was what they call 'background,' and he did more preparation than either of the two stars—combined. Their prep seemed to be limited to checking their touch ups before the makeup girl walked away," Erica said. "But the director had bigger ideas. Before filming began, they actually rehearsed. Well, maybe not the extras, I think they were on their own. The director is some little wunderkind. You know, the *really* creative type. It's his first film, so this time out, they're giving him whatever he wants. If the film isn't a huge success, they probably won't be quite as generous the next time. If there is a next time."

"How could it fail? It's got Alan, after all."

"It certainly has," said Erica. "And I have to say, I'm impressed by the cast."

"It's always good when one of the good guys makes it," said Dessie.

"Well, of course, I mean Alan. But beyond that casting coup, they seem to have chosen the supporting cast from theater, independent films, and episodes of *Law and Order*. You know, people who can really act."

"So it's a movie for theater people," said Dessie.

"Yes, it is," answered Erica. "And that's how I like it. Speaking of which, Alan did mention that you were an actress."

"I was, indeed," said Dessie. "Known professionally as Desmond Harris, if you can imagine. My parents had a strange sense of humor. They never said whether they wanted a boy or a girl. What they got was me, in all my glory. I'll admit to being short, and maybe a little less than picture perfect. But I can say with pride that I've taken parts away from other actresses, some of them who were, shall we say, babes. A long time ago, in another lifetime, I did Nora in *A Doll's House* Off-Broadway. That's where I met Alan, in fact. He was a wonderful Krogstad."

"Good to know that my man can be a convincing creep," said Erica.

"Redeemed by the love of a good woman in the end, don't forget," said Dessie.

"Isn't that always the way?" said Erica.

"And I did the aviatrix in Shaw's *Misalliance*, a part that almost always goes to a bigger girl, and Hermione in *Winter's Tale*. I guess it's easier for someone small to get up on that pedestal, but playing a statue is no piece of cake."

"I love that play, but I always thought Leontes was a jealous idiot," said Erica.

"Me too," Dessie said. "Then again, I married him."

"That's where you met your husband?"

"My dear Martin. The love of my life," sighed Dessie. "It may surprise you to know that I've had my share of relationships—"

"It doesn't," said Erica.

"Well, I'd been through one marriage that was over before the rice hit the ground, and then the one that took. Martin was it for me. We had two children, both adored. Then he died, suddenly. And I had two kids to raise by myself. I got the message pretty quickly that two children had to be fed more often than your average starving artist. I could type, not as fast as Claudia, but I had done lots of temp work—beats schlepping food or hustling drinks—and I got a job at the People's Theater. The pay was never great, but the check clears every week, and I'm still in the business. Maybe not on the front lines, but I'm still in the biz." As Dessie finished, she stabbed the last piece of avocado in her salad.

"It looks to me," said Erica, "like you're the power behind the throne."

"Alex is still the boss, but she trusts me to run the administrative end of things," said Dessie. "The hiring and so forth."

"Which explains me."

"The difference being that you came not only well recommended—by way of Alan—but with credits to boot."

"Outside of show biz, I think they're called credentials, Dessie."

"Whatever. We were pretty sure you would work out. Unlike some others."

"And what about the business end? I was supposed to meet the business manager when I came in for the interview, but he was out that day," said Erica.

"Oh, you haven't had the pleasure?" asked Dessie.

"That line reading could use a little more enthusiasm," said Erica.

"You're here for less than a day and you're giving line readings?" said Dessie. "We were right about you."

"And about the business manager?" asked Erica.

"Ron? Wait and see," said Dessie, taking a pained final sip of iced tea. "But enough of this work talk. Are you going to marry Alan?"

"Excuse me?" said Erica, taken aback by Dessie's question.

"I'm a mother, Erica. We ask these questions."

"Marriage, hmmm. Let's just say, 'it is an honor that I dream not of,'" answered Erica.

"Juliet!" said Dessie. "That's Juliet's line. And how do I know?"

"Let me guess," said Erica. "You played her."

"Of course I did. But back to my original question–"

"Marry Alan?" said Erica. "Ummm . . ."

"I see," said Dessie, pausing before her next question. "His fear of commitment?"

"If there's a commitment-phobe in this relationship, it's probably me."

"Do you want to have children?" Dessie continued, seemingly undaunted in her questioning.

"For the time being, I'd rather have thoughts," replied Erica.

"Okay, that takes care of that," Dessie announced, brushing her hands in a motion that said lunch and the questioning were over. "Let's settle up and get back. I don't want to leave Claudia alone for too long. She hasn't burned the place down yet, but let's not tempt fate."

"Okey dokey," said Erica. "We're off."

Erica's first afternoon at her job was spent tracking down just the right quotation for a congratulatory ad placed by the People's Theater in a program honoring a member of the Italian-American Alliance of Theater Professionals, "one in whom/The ancient Roman honour more appears/Than any that draws breath in Italy." Thank you, *Merchant of Venice*. Finding the quotation was not the hard part. The hard part was finding a copy of the *Shakespeare Concordance*, that repository of all quotations Shakespeare, organized according to topic. A perfunctory search unearthed not a single one in the building, which had housed more productions of Shakespeare's plays than any other in the city. (They did have several copies of the *Complete Works*, a volume that is organized by play title, not topic.) One of the advantages of being under Dessie's gentle supervision was that Erica could take a walk to the nearest library to find a concordance, quickly skim the index for the word "Italy," find the apt quotation, then take her time walking back on a beautiful September afternoon, with no one asking where she had been or why she hadn't simply looked as far as the computer on her desk to find the information online. If Day One was any indication, the real challenge for Erica would be filling the hours rather fulfilling the job requirements.

As she returned to her office, Erica heard a familiar tune being warbled from the direction of Dessie's office.

"Happy Birthday, dear Claudia. Happy Birthday to you!"

Erica followed the sound. She watched from outside the door as Claudia, seated at her desk, stared shyly into her lap. Dessie and two young women whom Erica had yet to meet stood over her desk. Either it was dress-up day or Erica had located two of the trust-fund babies in casual but unmistakably expensive khaki pants and tailored white linen shirts—designer labels and 'dry clean only.' They were both tall and thin—Chloe was black and Asha was white—the absolute equivalent of each other. Above Claudia's head, Dessie held a white-frosted chocolate cupcake with a candle burning in the center. When the serenade ended, she placed it before Claudia.

"Make a wish," said Dessie. Claudia immediately squeezed her eyes shut and blew out the candle, after some difficulty in locating the target and avoiding the flame. With the mission accomplished, Chloe and Asha quickly fled, their eye contact with Dessie suggesting that they had been pressed into service, and some little reward had been offered and would be forthcoming.

"Thank you, ladies," said Dessie.

"Later, Dessie," they chimed.

The two left the office without acknowledging Claudia, who didn't seem to notice, cementing Erica's sense that the event, like so many others in this building, had been staged. It was the People's Theater, after all. Erica returned to her seat to fashion an activity that would keep her looking busy for the remainder of the afternoon.

A few hours after that, she arrived home.

"So, how was your first day?" asked Alan.

"Daddy's home," sang Erica. "And before me. To what do we owe the pleasure?"

"Technical difficulties. Do you want to hear about it?"

"Not really," she said.

"Well, then, did you play nice with the other children?" Alan gently inquired.

"*Children* being the operative word," said Erica. "They have a whole lot of young ones around that place. All of them eager."

"You're not exactly ancient, my dear," said Alan.

"And not exactly eager," said Erica.

"Thank God for that. Did the young ones remind you of your students?"

"*Former* students," said Erica, with emphasis. "And no, not really. First of all, these guys are a little older. Secondly, working at the People's Theater is really a feather in the cap of these up and comers. They seem to share an attitude that says 'we made it.' For a number of my former students, it was more of a world-weary 'we made it this far.'"

"A subtle difference," said Alan.

"Not really," Erica replied. "And these children like to promenade in pairs, talking on their phones. I prefer to think they're not talking to each other."

"So, that's their story. What's yours?"

"Well," said Erica, "for some reason one is expected to sit there all day, work or no work."

"Imagine that," said Alan, feigning surprise. "And how did you like Dessie?"

"We bonded over *The Brothers Wittgenstein* this morning, and then moved on to lunch."

"Sounds promising," said Alan.

"We're still finding our rhythm, but so far, so good," said Erica.

"It seems like you're finding it pretty quickly," replied Alan. "With such a beginning, who knows what tomorrow will bring?"

"One of Dessie's favorite topics is her late husband, Martin," Erica began. "Or, should I say, the sainted Martin. You knew him well?"

"Well enough. Martin McNulty was an okay guy and an okay actor. But he was no saint."

"Oh, really?" asked Erica.

"Let's just say, he got around before he met Dessie."

"And after?"

"Not that I heard. Then again, I wasn't keeping score," said Alan.

"She seems to think the sun rose and set on him. How did he die? She didn't say and I didn't ask," Erica replied.

"Martin had some kind of heart problem that they knew nothing about until it killed him. He just dropped dead one day."

"Wow, that can't have been easy. For anyone."

"To tell you the truth, I always thought Dessie would be the one to have the career," said Alan. "But she's got those kids to raise. One of them was an infant when Martin died. How old are they now?"

Erica grimaced. "I was supposed to ask that, wasn't I?"

"That is the generally accepted custom," said Alan. "Now for the bonus question. Does she have a boy? A girl?"

"Probably?" said Erica, stretching out the syllables.

Alan made a buzzer noise. "I'm sorry, we cannot accept that answer. The correct answer is one of each." He gave her a look of concern. "Come on, Erica. I know you have social skills, try as you might to hide them. And you'll be looking at these people for about eight hours a day."

"First of all, most of these people are located on the other side of the building, where they sit in cubicles—

no doubt, adding new meaning to the term 'pod people.'

"And my office, I'll have you know, is on the side of the building where we have actual doors. And a window. Okay, it faces a brick wall, but hopeful realtors would say that the light is, if not excellent, then, existent. So I don't have to talk to anyone I don't want to."

"Oh, yes, you do," was Alan's simple response.

"Okay, maybe I do," Erica agreed begrudgingly. "But being the new girl in town, I'll wait till they come to me. Which Dessie says they will, to figure out what, if anything, I can do for their careers. Once they see that the answer is a resounding *nothing,* that will be that."

"Fine, do it your way," said Alan, returning to his task.

"What are you doing, by the way?" asked Erica.

"I'm cleaning out the refrigerator."

"So I see. The food all over the counter was my first clue."

"Nothing gets by you. Do you remember that day a while back when we both decided to eat healthy?"

"Vaguely."

"There's something here wrapped in aluminum foil. It appears to be green. I'm guessing a vegetable."

"Did it start out green or did it achieve greenness?" asked Erica.

"I think that it started and stayed green," Alan replied.

"Yes, now it's coming back to me," said Erica. "I'm pretty sure it's broccoli, and it isn't getting any younger."

"Neither are we," said Alan.

"Let's eat out," suggested Erica.

"Is that your answer to everything?" he asked.

"It works in so many contexts," Erica answered. "And I think we need to celebrate my return to the work force."

A short time later, Erica found herself seated at another outdoor café, this one serving Italian food. She sipped a perspiring glass of pinot grigio as she waited for the antipasto to appear.

"Erica, now that you've gotten through the first day, maybe you can explain to me what you're doing at the People's Theater," Alan began.

"You want a job description?"

"No," said Alan, "I want you to explain why you took a job for which you're overqualified."

"*Vastly* overqualified," said Erica.

"And which doesn't pay all that well."

"Peanuts. And we've been through this before, Alan," said Erica, with more than a little emphasis on his name. "It's temporary, until I make up my mind what I want to do next."

"And as I've said to you before, you could make your way back into advertising, where the bigger bucks are. The place you lived before your foray into teaching," said Alan.

"Spoken like a true artist. Yes, Alan, I know. But I think I'll try this for a while. I take a certain pride in the fact that, at the People's Theater, I'm the go-to girl when a semi-colon crisis rears its ugly head."

"That's the gig?" asked Alan.

"They're counting on me," said Erica, reaching for a bread stick, which she snapped in two. "It's important that they know that punctuation is our friend."

"So I've heard," said Alan. "But are you sure about this?"

"Yes. For the time being, yes," she insisted. "After all, I'm the person who sits at the elbow of the person who sits at the elbow of the person who makes the big decisions. Actually, there may be another elbow in there, but no one knows what she does. So, can we ease off this topic and enjoy another dinner that I am not cooking?"

"Gladly. And when was the last time you cooked dinner?" asked Alan.

"My point exactly," she said.

"Just one more thing on the subject of work," said Alan. "Have you heard from the folks at your previous place of employ—"

"No," said Erica, cutting him off. "They don't write, they don't call, and I don't care."

Erica had recently left a teaching position after a little unpleasantness in the English Department.

Alan persevered. "Not even your friend Sarah?"

"Not a word, not a syllable. I think I don't miss her most of all," Erica replied. "They all kind of left it with a 'Don't let the screen door hit you on the way out.'"

"That's not how I remember it," said Alan. "They did offer you continued employment."

"Which came with strings," Erica said. "And we're not talking twine. Cords—cables, actually." Erica paused. "Are you suggesting that I go back?"

"Of course not. But it never hurts to consider the alternatives," said Alan.

Erica looked shocked. "What?" she asked, after a moment had elapsed. "And leave show biz?"

CHAPTER 2

"I'm nobody! Who are you?
Are you—nobody—too?"
Emily Dickinson

By the next morning, Erica might have reconsidered her decision not to leave show business, which surrounded her in all its various forms. When her alarm went off, Alan was in the shower, readying himself for the day's filming. Just as Erica was struggling to consciousness, the phone rang. From under the covers, she reached out to grab the receiver in order to stop the ringing. She should have let it be.

At the other end of the phone, a voice, distinctly female, cooed, "Is Alan there?"

Not the best way to start the day. And this was the way the day had started for more mornings than Erica cared to count.

"Hello, Jenn. It's Erica. Alan's in the shower," she said, as if by rote.

"I'll wait," said Jenn, audibly disappointed.

"You can't, Jenn," said Erica, who was practiced at these games. "I'm expecting an important call. And we don't have call waiting."

"Maybe you should get it," Jenn offered, hopefully.

"Just give me the message, Jenn."

"Okay," she said reluctantly. "Tell Alan, his pick up is delayed by twenty minutes. But I promise to be there to get him."

"I know you will," said Erica. "Bye now."

"And tell him—"

"Got it," said Erica as she put down the receiver.

By this time, Alan had emerged from the bathroom, wrapped in a towel and a shroud of steam.

"Let me guess," he said, having seen Erica replace the receiver with more force than was needed.

"Alan, dear, that was your favorite production assistant—and mine, too—letting you know that the car will be twenty minutes late picking you up. But she's commandeered a driver, possibly at gun point, and will be here, come hell or high water," said Erica.

"Thanks for the message. Sorry if she woke you up," replied Alan, toweling his hair as he prepared to dress.

"Not a problem, I was almost conscious. But more to the point, does that girl understand that I am the obstacle in the path of her happiness?"

"Erica, she's a PA. It's just a crush."

"She knows I exist," said Erica. "She even knows my name. Which she refuses to use, by the way."

"She knows your name," said Alan. "And she knows where you live. You might want to remember that. Jenn strikes me as a very determined girl."

"Don't think you're off the hook," said Erica. "Those very determined types don't take rejection all that well. They can turn on you in a minute and do all sorts of nasty things with sharp, pointy objects."

"I'm not too worried," said Alan. "If this is a crush, she seems to be working it from afar. From the other end of the phone—"

"From the other end of the front seat," said Erica. "Not a lot of distance there."

"Believe me, when filming is over, Jenn will move on to another job and another unrequited love," said Alan. "I get the impression that she does this on every set."

"How did you get so lucky? Let me guess. She saw you in *Othello* in Central Park. She loved you as Iago because she likes bad boys. Very bad boys."

"Iago is no boy," said Alan. "And Jenn is a movie girl, not a theater buff. Movie people usually give you their condolences when they hear that you've done a lot of theater. 'Six performances a week? Outdoors? In the rain? For scale?' They think we need our heads examined. So I don't think there's any reason to worry."

"I'm not worried," said Erica brightly. "I'm not the one she adores."

Things did not improve by the time Erica got to work. Heeding Dessie's warning about Claudia's coffee, she bought her ration from the Starbucks across from the People's Theater. The Starbucks on the northwest corner, not the one diagonally across the street. The tactic proved unnecessary, given that when Erica got upstairs, neither Claudia nor the coffee was in evidence. Her own foamy brew would keep Erica awake and possibly occupied if there were no grammatical crisis on the horizon. She was mindful of the need to look busy, but still not quite sure how this need would be met.

Another introduction was about to take place.

"So you are Erica," said the tall male figure that uncoiled as he leaned over her desk, delivering his line as if it were a pointed comment.

"Vain to deny it," Erica replied. "And you are?"

He looked as if she should be well aware of the answer to this question. But he deigned to reply.

"I'm Ron Vartan. Business manager of the People's Theater." Ron looked as though the next words out of his mouth would be "Your boss," but he held back.

Even after a short time on the job, Erica knew the chain of command.

"I was looking for you yesterday, but you were out," Ron said.

"Good morning, Ron," said Dessie, in a singsong voice that revealed no hint of pleasure. She stood behind him, though not visible behind his hulking form. "How are we this morning?"

"We are fine, thank you, Dessie." Ron turned to meet his questioner, while Erica quickly leaned sideways and mouthed a grateful "Thank you" from behind his back, before resuming her position. Dessie saw this and winked.

"I need to talk to Alex this morning," Ron said in a tone that revealed more about his self-importance than the need for this meeting. "We have to discuss the figures for the Michelangelo project. We cannot let costs go through the roof."

"I bet she knows that, Ron," said Dessie. "Yes, I think she's probably well aware of the need for fiscal restraint. But she was out yesterday, as you know, and this morning she has meetings scheduled with the design team, followed by more meetings with the director and possible cast members. If we can't get this thing cast, then it won't cost us a penny because there will be no show."

Ron looked increasingly annoyed as Dessie made her way through the litany of Alex's appointments.

"I thought that's what auditions were for," said Ron, with a sneer in his voice.

"Absolutely right, Ron," replied Dessie, ignoring his tone. "But these little chats are for the name players. With the name recognition that might get people into the theater. You know, the stars of stage, screen, and television."

"Especially television," said Dessie, bending around Ron to include Erica in the conversation. "That's why it's called show business, Ron, not show art."

"I know what it's called," Ron snapped. "Just keep in mind that if we blow our budget on this production, then we won't have enough left to renovate that theater upstairs. You know, the one you're so keen on naming."

Dessie summoned all of her nearly five-foot frame and fixed Ron with a look that could politely be described as hard. Then, just as quickly, she relented.

"Ron, my friend, for you I'll find room. I promise."

Ron looked ready for more of a fight but quickly took "yes" for an answer.

"Thank you, Dessie," he said, with faint satisfaction. "I'll be in my office, whenever you're ready for me," he continued, spinning on his heel to exit before she changed her mind. He left with no word for Erica.

"I'll find you," called Dessie cheerfully to Ron's departing back. Once he was gone, Dessie turned to Erica. "I just saved you from an inquisition," she said.

"All I can say is thank you," said Erica.

"Don't be too pleased," said Dessie. "Sooner or later, he'll want to know whatever he can worm out of you. I think he keeps a file on everyone, though I can't prove it. Just a feeling."

"I could believe that," said Erica. "He has a way about him that suggests covert operations."

"Yes," said Dessie, "the CIA's loss is our gain. Although he will want to know all about you, you may be relieved to know that his interest is strictly professional."

"That beard is too well-tended to suggest anything else," said Erica. "Is he *trying* to look satanic?"

"Most of the effect is studied, I think, but that may just come naturally. And, of course, tell him nothing," said Dessie. "He will want to know why we hired you, since he had nothing to do with that particular decision."

"*That* would be a question better directed at the person who did the hiring."

"It has been," said Dessie. "I told him that we were lucky to get you. Beyond that, I don't have time for explanations." Dessie looked at her watch. "I'll leave him to count beans for most of the day and lord it over the poor children in his sector. As you may have noticed, his office is on the other side of the building."

"Your doing?" asked Erica.

"Alex's actually. To which I gave a hearty thumbs up. I mean, somebody has to torment, I mean, watch over the future of the American Theater."

"The poor dears," said Erica.

"Hopefully, he's not over there bouncing them on his knee. But if they can survive Ron, they can survive anything," Dessie rationalized. "I'll squeeze him in for a short meeting with Alex late this afternoon. Just to keep him happy."

"Dessie, I can see that you're very good at what you do."

"Yes, I am. And one more thing, Erica. I haven't said anything about your connection to Alan. I mean, around here, we think of him as one of ours, since he got his big break in one of our productions."

In the halls of the People's Theater, the recent good fortune of Alan DeLorme was spoken of in reverential tones. His role as Iago in the People's production of *Othello* had catapulted him from working actor to *movie star*, depending on whom you asked. The truth was a little less star struck, but he had a nice role in his first feature film, and that was nothing to sneeze at.

"I didn't plan to present Alan as your claim to fame," Dessie continued. "I'll leave it up to you to say as much or as little as you want about your personal life."

"Thanks, Dessie. I've been living out of town for a couple of years, so I hadn't really thought of myself as an extension of Alan."

"I didn't mean to suggest—" said Dessie hastily.

"No, no offense," said Erica. "Really, none taken. I think I'll let them be dazzled by my charm before I trade on my connection to Alan."

"I thought that's what you'd want," answered Dessie. "Now where is that girl?"

"Here, Dessie," said Claudia, racing into the office with her marble notebook gripped tightly in her hand, her large black shoulder bag flying. She stopped abruptly in front of Dessie. "I'm sorry," she said. "There was a delay on the train."

"Another one?" asked Dessie, briefly waving at Erica as she led Claudia back into their office. "Claudia, we have a full day, so let's get moving."

"Yes, Dessie," said Claudia, following her like a duckling to her desk.

CHAPTER 3

"Here come real stars to fill the upper skies,
And here on earth come emulating flies"
Robert Frost, "Fireflies in the Garden"

Later that morning, Erica looked up from her desk to see a woman standing by the coffee machine on the other side of the room. Alexa Wallace looked skeptically at the brew that Claudia had concocted. Even fresh, it still looked, and, Erica guessed, tasted, like mud. As the new employee, Erica thought it a good time to make her presence felt. She got up from her desk and crossed the floor to say hi to the boss.

The boss turned to greet her.

"Erica," she said, "how nice to see you again. I'm so glad you decided to join us."

To Erica, this sounded as though she had agreed to fill out a foursome for a round of golf.

The speaker continued in this vein. "I'm so sorry I wasn't here to greet you on your first day. Is Dessie taking good care of you?"

Now she is the maître d' and Dessie is my waiter, thought Erica.

"Dessie's been great," Erica said. "She's been showing me the ropes. And explaining everything."

"If there's anything Dessie can't answer—which I doubt—feel free to ask me."

"Thank you, Alexa, I will," said Erica.

"Oh, please, call me Alex. Everyone does. Yes, Dessie knows everything about everything."

"Absolutely," Erica said. An awkward pause followed, which Erica filled with "Did you enjoy your day off?"

"It was fine," said Alex, a flicker of emotion interrupting her noncommittal expression. "I think I'll pass on the coffee," she said, quickly turning and moving in the direction of her office. Then she stopped, turned back to Erica, and said,

"We're very pleased that you're here with us. Again, welcome."

"Thank you," said Erica, no closer to deciding what to make of the boss. Alex's greeting seemed genuine, even if the smile that accompanied it didn't quite meet her eyes.

Alex retreated to her office, passing Claudia on the way. Although Claudia was already on her way out and probably had the right of way, she stood aside as Alex marched past her without a look in her direction. Erica, still standing in the foyer, watched a storm cloud of emotions pass across Claudia's face. Her first reaction at the proximity of Alex seemed to be one of awe mixed with a heavy dose of intimidation. As Alex brushed by her without a word, Claudia shifted to annoyance, her irritation giving way to anger. The speed of her emotions slowed at the unexpected sound of Dessie's voice, followed by Dessie herself.

"Claudia," said Dessie, snapping out her name. "Oh, hi, Erica," she added.

Erica was still looking at Claudia, who had a few more emotions in her rapid-fire arsenal. Rage was what Erica saw blazing up, and then, just as swiftly, the fire was out, replaced by her habitual look of befuddlement.

"Don't just stand there, Claudia," said Dessie. "Let's get a move on. Where were you going?"

"Nowhere, Dessie," said Claudia, once again the obedient child.

"You're holding a pile of papers, Claudia," Dessie continued. "They must go somewhere."

"Oh, yes," said Claudia, suddenly alert. "Be right back, Dessie," she said, racing off to parts unknown. She swerved around Erica and was out of the office before Dessie could question her further.

"I don't know what I'm going to do with that girl," Dessie said, exhaling a long, slow sigh.

Erica shrugged. "I guess we'll see," she said.

Thinking this would be a fine time to take her own walk around the building, Erica decided that, if anyone asked, she was familiarizing herself with her new surroundings. Her true agenda was simply to stretch her legs and leave the tiny box that was her home for eight hours a day—door or no door. Another trip to the library was out of the question, at least for today. Now that introductions had been made, Ron struck her as watchful.

Spanning five floors, with the administrative offices wedged on either side of the second floor, the People's Theater was not one but several theaters—seven and counting—of varying sizes and shapes, spread out across the building. Some of the performance spaces had fancy proscenium arches, while others had a stage in the middle of the floor, surrounded by seats that could best be described as well worn and, at times, mildly painful. The People's Theater didn't discriminate: classic plays, contemporary drama, the famous and the infamous, all found a place. All they had to do was get in the door.

But not every theatergoer, even the most intrepid, could be expected to climb four flights to discover the newest voice in the American Theater. So, an elevator had been installed to ease the journey.

Erica usually took the stairs, but, to learn every aspect of the People's Theater, she decided to give the elevator a try. Much to her surprise, when the elevator doors opened, Claudia was standing inside.

"Getting out?" asked Erica, given that this was Claudia's floor.

"I'm not going back to the office just yet," Claudia replied.

A kindred spirit, Erica thought, asking, "Where are you going?"

"I just pressed down," said Claudia.

"Okay, then," Erica said. "Down it is."

The elevator immediately went up.

Erica looked at Claudia, who stared straight ahead, seemingly unaware that they were moving in the wrong direction. At the third floor, a group of young men, all carrying lighting equipment, trundled into the elevator. Erica volunteered to get out, but they insisted that there was room for everyone. No one spoke to Claudia or seemed to notice that she was there. She responded in kind.

As the elevator now moved slowly downward, the lighting technicians joked amongst themselves. Beneath the sound of their commentary, Erica could make out, just barely, another voice speaking quietly. She turned to look at Claudia, who was talking to no one in particular. Or, more precisely, she was moving her lips. Her hair masked most of the conversation, which went unnoticed by the other occupants, who spilled out at the first floor. Erica decided that she had seen enough of the elevator for the time being.

"I think I'll go back to my office," said Erica, moving to get out.

"Me too," said Claudia, pushing the button before Erica had a chance to escape.

"Okay, then," said Erica, retreating to the back left corner of the elevator, leaving the panel of buttons in Claudia's care.

Claudia returned to her mild trance and continued to say whatever it was she was saying to herself.

Is she praying? Erica wondered.

The elevator slowly returned to the second floor. This little adventure had given Erica one more good reason to take the stairs. Claudia exited the elevator, saying nothing to Erica, who followed her back to the office at a safe distance.

A few hours later, Erica had a chance to confer with Dessie when Claudia had been sent to the copy room with a large stack of papers.

"Is Claudia an actress?" Erica asked.

"God, I hope not," said Dessie. "Why do you ask?"

"I took a short ride with her on the elevator, and she spent the whole time mumbling to herself. She was either memorizing lines or practicing incantations."

"I vote for the second one, definitely," said Dessie. "Did she say anything to you?"

"No, just the mumbling to herself."

"Well, that's our Claudia," said Dessie. "I would ask if she seemed to be under the influence of anything, but I don't think that's likely. Other than youthful enthusiasm, of course."

"Claudia doesn't seem all that enthused," said Erica. "And how old is she anyway?"

"I don't know, offhand," said Dessie. "In her low-to-mid-twenties, I assume. Just like the rest of them. Or at least, that's what they admit to. I can check if you're curious. Human Resources would know. I see everyone's information when they're hired—birthdays and so on—but those are quickly forgotten."

"You remembered Claudia's birthday," said Erica. "I saw the cupcake celebration."

"Well, that was different," said Dessie. "She doesn't seem to have any friends at the theater or in New York, for that matter, and not likely to make any, for reasons that may be obvious. So I took pity on her. It was only a cupcake."

"You're just a big softie, Dessie," said Erica.

"If you say so," said Dessie. "Now I have a project for you."

"I have one question," asked Erica.

"But I haven't described the project yet," said Dessie.

"No, not about that," Erica replied. "It's something Ron said. I've been meaning to ask you. What's all this I hear about you naming theaters?"

"Oh, yes, Ron and his subtle form of blackmail. Instead of naming our latest performance space after someone rich or famous, Alex has decided that the two new theaters will be named after a couple of the unsung heroes of the theater world. Working actors who never got the recognition they deserved. Alex has promised me that one of the theaters will be named after my late husband, Martin."

"Dessie, that's wonderful," said Erica, genuinely impressed. "You must be so pleased."

"Oh, I'm thrilled," said Dessie. "Beyond words. I haven't told the kids, because there's no need to get them excited in case it all falls apart. You just never know. But there's nothing I wouldn't do to see this project through."

"I'm sure," said Erica.

"Now all we have to do is find the funding for the renovations," said Dessie. "Which explains Ron and his comments about the cost of the next production."

"Oh, I expect that nothing truly explains Ron," said Erica.

"That may be," Dessie replied. "But it's a cruel fact of life that every non-profit theater is in search of the next big hit, just like the commercial houses. And as a non-profit theater, we get tax-exempt status, which just kills the commercial producers, poor babies. If we have any extra money lying around, it goes to fund the next production, and to pay our piddling salaries, of course. Government agencies and foundations, they still give, but in this economy, not nearly as much. As for the individual donors, well, the stock market has been playing some nasty tricks on our most loyal friends. We had a great run with *The Bros*, but we need something new to fill the coffers."

"And to build your theater?" Erica asked.

"That too," said Dessie.

"Okay, so it's on to the project," said Erica. "What do you want me to do?"

The army of the ambitious might come in all colors, shapes, and sizes, but they shared a single goal: to change the face of American Theater. They differed on what that fabulous face would look like when they finished with it and how fast the change would take place. Some were fine with the approach taken by the People's Theater. Even when the theater alternated a classic play with the contemporary mix, it tended to take the most innovative approach imaginable, or, in some cases, unimaginable, as productions of Shakespeare set on Mars would come to prove.

Those within the army of the ambitious were too mindful of their careers to raise any real objections, but there was always some dissention within the ranks. Asha and Chloe might glide about the place in full agreement with the way things worked at the People's Theater, the rules always having worked for them, why would they stop now? Beyond those who would take the more gradual approach to infusing change into the American Theater, there were others who would make that change with a large mallet, and immediately. There was no telling if the patient would survive after this speedy operation, but they were more than willing to give it a try.

Zack, Zeke, and Christy, two guys and a girl, all in their twenties, were one such subset.

They traveled as a pack whenever they could escape their desks and the watchful eye of Ron. Zack had the bright red hair that was supposed to match his temperament, while Christy, with her tangled web of dirty blonde hair, and Zeke, with his dark Mediterranean looks, followed Zack, their alpha dog, wherever he would go. The cutting edge was too tame for them and the avant-garde was old hat, their favorite play among recent offerings being one in which a few of the roles were assigned to inanimate objects (a lamp, a table, a chair) with actors speaking the lines from an offstage location.

How they planned to achieve an overthrow of the current state of things was more of a mystery. Rising in the hierarchy of the People's Theater would be a start, but they had to bide their time, something for which Zack, in particular, lacked the patience, choosing instead to be pro-active. He took a long, hard look at the available talent to determine who was the most expendable. He fastened upon Claudia.

Dessie may have spent most of her days trying to figure out why Claudia inhabited the desk next to hers, but to Zack it was unfathomable. Proximity to the seat of power was crucial to Zack's plan, and Claudia was already there, wasting space. Undermining her was futile because Claudia had that covered; she undermined herself. So Zack took the unusual route of engaging Claudia directly. And curiously, although seemingly oblivious to her surroundings, she engaged him right back.

"Still here?" said Zack to Claudia as he unceremoniously dumped several file folders on her desk, with Zeke and Christy in tow, as mostly silent onlookers.

"And you aren't," replied Claudia, giving him as direct a look as she could from behind her bangs.

"But for how long?" asked Zack, as he backed out of the room, taking his followers with him.

"Totally," said Christy.

"Good one," chimed in Zeke.

"Long enough," said Claudia, as she looked down at her work, dismissing them in her own way.

Dessie and Erica had been sitting in Erica's office at the time of this exchange but close enough to hear it take place.

"What's that about?" asked Erica, as she discreetly closed her door before hearing the answer.

"Zack seems to think that the way to advance in this place is to bug the person whose seat you want. I won't say harass; it isn't that aggressive and Claudia is playing along. It's not as if the three of them are ganging up on her since two of them have almost nothing to say. They're just along for the ride, and she ignores them anyway. And since he's the only person she seems to connect with, even in this weird and unusual way, I have no plans to step in. And while I may have serious doubts about Claudia sitting in that seat, Zack has no chance. I've heard his rant on the state of the theater as we know it. I have no plans to hear it on a continual loop."

"As mating calls go, 'Are you still here?' is one of the odder ones I've heard," said Erica. "But their banter, minus the wit, could indicate they had some sort of strange attraction to each other."

"Doubtful," replied Dessie.

"Since neither one is a middle schooler working on a first crush, you're probably right," said Erica.

"Let's not insult middle schoolers in love," said Dessie. "That's my son Luke's ball park," she continued.

"Has Luke discovered girls?" asked Erica.

"No," Dessie answered, "they have discovered him."

"I'm not surprised," Erica offered.

"Just like his daddy," Dessie sighed.

I hope not, thought Erica, a thought she kept to herself.

CHAPTER 4

"I saw the angel in the marble and carved until I set him free."
Michelangelo

"First of all, I must swear you to secrecy."

"Consider me duly sworn," said Alan, seated at the kitchen table, sipping a beer.

"We're putting on a play," said Erica.

"At the People's Theater? I didn't see that one coming."

Erica chose to ignore his sarcasm. "It's a play with music."

"Well, that's different," he admitted.

"It's a different kind of musical. Nothing too blatantly commercial, which wouldn't go with the non-profit vibe that ricochets off the walls down there."

"Wouldn't wanna harm your street cred," said Alan, giving Erica more to ignore.

"They're looking for that magical combination of artistic triumph and money maker," she said.

"And what is the subject of your little play, I mean, play with music?" asked Alan.

"Wait. Are you ready?" Alan nodded, a little too eagerly to be convincing. "It's Michelangelo. *Michelangelo: The Musical*," Erica said with some satisfaction.

"*The* Michelangelo? The painter, the sculptor—"

"The architect, the engineer. He even wrote a sonnet or two."

"And he sings?" asked Alan.

"This one will," Erica answered.

"I guess there's nothing that can't be put through the musicalizer," Alan said. "And DaVinci's been done."

"Done to dead," agreed Erica. "So why not move on to his chief rival?"

"Sounds good to me," said Alan. "But why all the secrecy?"

"Well, Dessie says that the project has to remain secret for the time being. All that's known, and only by a very few, is that there's a project and that it's about Michelangelo."

"Hon, all over New York, even as we speak, people are swearing each other to secrecy," Alan insisted.

"Maybe they are, but the People's people still don't want the information leaking out. They haven't cast it yet, and the director, the script, the songs, everything is very hush hush."

"Top secret has a very short shelf life in the theater, Erica. Somebody will get hired and tell his or her significant other, who will tell someone else, and so on and so on—"

"Agreed," said Erica. "But for the moment, nobody is supposed to be talking."

"Except you, apparently," said Alan. "And what is your role in this? Have you been cast as his wife? His mother? His young grandmother?"

"I'll leave the acting right where it belongs, thank you. And to save you blushes, your name has already been mentioned as a possible Michelangelo."

"You've heard me sing, right?"

"Yes, but apparently they haven't, so you're still in the running," Erica said. "And the big guy must have had a mother," she continued, "maybe even a grandmother. But his romantic choices did not tend in the direction of the ladies."

"Not the marrying kind?" asked Alan.

"Not unless civil unions were all the rage in Renaissance Italy. He had an eye for male beauty—check out his sculptures if you have any doubt—and he did have an older man/younger man thing going on when he was 57—"

"I hope he was the older man," said Alan.

"He was," replied Erica, a little testily. "His most serious beau was 23 when they met, the recipient of the aforementioned sonnets. There's still some debate among scholars as to whether his interest in young men was of the erotic or the platonic variety. Possibly both."

"Well, they can't all have been surrogate sons," said Alan.

"Oh, they weren't," Erica replied, "a topic I'm sure they'll cover in Act II. During their duet, no doubt. There were a number of young men in Michelangelo's life, most of whom showed their devotion to him by stealing his work and selling it. Even so, or maybe because of this, our Mike was a very private person. But the serious boyfriend—Tomassino Somebody—was true blue and loyal to him."

"So he was in love with a wonderful guy—named Tomassino," said Alan. "I feel a love song coming on."

"Just as long as you keep it to yourself," said Erica.

"Is there a plot?" asked Alan.

"His life, his loves, his art. With song and dance. Isn't that enough?" replied Erica to his question.

"We still haven't discovered your role in all this," said Alan.

"Oh, me? Well, I've been chosen to serve as the resident Michelangelo expert."

"Wait a minute," said Alan. "How are you pronouncing his name?"

"As the resident expert, I should pronounce it Mickle-angelo. His full name was Michelangelo di Lodovico Buonarroti Simoni. So, repeat after me—"

"No, thank you," said Alan.

"Well, now that we know we've been mispronouncing Godot all these years," Erica said. "It's *God*-ot. I just wanted to alert you to the fashionable way to say Mikey's name."

"I think I'll stick with the peasant pronunciation," Alan said. "And with all the museums in all of New York, they decided you were the right one for the job?"

"I too shared your skepticism when Dessie told me," said Erica, "but it depends on what your definition of 'expert' is. Do they want someone who's spent several decades studying Michelangelo's art and every last detail of his life? Noooo. What they want is a general outline of Mikey's dates and places and the names that go with them. If a question comes up at rehearsal over some historical detail, I make a quick trip to the library or the internet to answer it. I'm on call for any and all such emergencies."

"That's usually what a dramaturg does," offered Alan.

"Yes," said Erica, "and they don't have to hire a dramaturg if they already have me on the payroll. I think I can balance this task with my semi-colon duties."

"And somewhere out there is one more unemployed dramaturg," Alan began.

"So what else is new?" Erica finished. "At least things are finally getting interesting at work," she said.

"It's about time," said Alan. "You've been there for almost a week."

"Exactly," said Erica. "I haven't seen a copy of the script—I think it's under lock and key—and they never let the staff anywhere near rehearsals. So we dine on any morsel that drops from the table. But this thing is definitely in the works."

Erica paused, for dramatic effect. "And I saved the best for last. Starting next week, to create interest in a project that is supposed to be top secret, everyone at the People's Theater will be wearing buttons announcing the production."

"Buttons that announce a secret production?" asked Alan.

"Yes," said Erica. "Brilliant, isn't it? The catch phrase, the slogan, whatever you want to call it, will be the only official word on the production."

"Don't keep me in suspense," said Alan. "And the button will read?"

"I like Mike," said Erica.

"I'm sure you do," said Alan. "But what's the catch phrase?"

"You heard me," Erica said.

"Did you write that?" he asked.

"I wish I had," she answered.

CHAPTER 5

"From our birthday, until we die,
Is but the winking of an eye."
William Butler Yeats

Walking into a new job, Erica knew she was entering a story already in progress. The major players had been established; the lines had been set and drawn. Now, what role would she play? Would she start out as an extra and stay there? Would she be promoted to featured player? Would they spin her off to a series of her own, or would she find herself cancelled after only a few episodes?

As the weeks passed at the People's Theater, Erica chose to stay in the back, a supernumerary hugging the scenery. She played her role diligently. Given the relative unimportance of correct punctuation to the American Theater, Erica regularly escaped her cinderblock cell to do her research at the local library, the walk to and from being far more essential than the knowledge to be gained there. But someone else's plans changed all that, and she found herself playing a more prominent part than she'd ever envisioned.

Even at the People's Theater, a theater lobby can be a lonely place, especially when emptied of the critics who come to praise or to blame, the janitor sweeping out yesterday's opinions, and most importantly, the theatergoers, hoping to answer life's questions or question life's answers, all in the space of an evening. Were it not for the fact that the theater was dark on that Monday night, the lobby might have echoed with judgments made and in the making, but there was no one there to hear them. No one except strange, quiet Claudia. Her way of being in the world was to stay out of everyone's way, but in doing so, she managed to be in everyone's way. So it was with her death. Late on a Tuesday morning, Claudia was found seated on the floor of the lobby, propped up in a corner, not quite hidden by a display counter. Her vacant stare had, at one time or another, perplexed nearly everyone who met her; now, it was completely appropriate to her situation and surroundings.

Apparently, the secret of *Michelangelo: The Musical* was not safe with anyone. Either that, or a fan of the ceiling at the Sistine Chapel had decided to create his or her own version of Michelangelo's *The Creation of Man*. In keeping with the surroundings, Claudia's body had been staged. Like Adam reaching out to touch the hand of God, Claudia had been posed to point her fingers at an unseen deity, with her left leg bent in a position that a Pilates instructor would admire. Unlike Adam, who appears as God made him in the painting, Claudia was dressed in the same drab outfit—faded jeans, wilted tee shirt—that she had worn to work the day before, hinting that she never left the building after the work day was done. Now, all her days were done. But unlike Adam, Claudia could no longer sit up to copy his languorous pose, so she leaned for support on the display case, her body listing to one side, her head tilted upward at the lobby's less-than-Sistine ceiling of molded tin.

A blow to the head rarely causes sudden death. Sadly for Claudia, there was no figure of God by her side to restore life as it drained away. The point of departure was an indentation at the base of her skull. The dent in her skull matched the bottom of the object encircled by Claudia's right hand. When separated from her fingers, it was confirmed as a Kemby Award, Broadway's biggest prize, named for Fanny Kemble, the nineteenth century actress and oldest daughter of a renowned theatrical family, who gained her own fame performing the major roles in Shakespeare's plays and as the author of her own. Many would kill for a Kemby, but to kill with a Kemby? This alone showed the kind of ingenuity that wins awards. In some circles, it would be applauded.

The statuette gripped by Claudia was the property of the People's Theater. Nearly a decade before, *The Brothers Wittgenstein* had swept all the awards for which it had been nominated, including the Kemby for Best Musical. Usually this award, among others, resided in a glass case in the producer's office. The office was supposed to be locked at night, but the case, never. Not that anyone made a habit of coming in and handling the Kemby, in preparation for that day when the holder might have one of his or her own. But in keeping with the tenets of the People's Theater, the award belonged to the people, to the People's people, even if they could only admire it from afar. Now, it appeared that someone had found another use for the People's Kemby.

It was unlikely that Claudia could have done the deed herself. A self-administered blow to the back of her head would be awkward enough, and this one came with more force and feeling than Claudia had ever shown in the span of her short life and shorter time at the People's Theater. The traces of Claudia on the statuette, mostly hair and a little bit of skull, could not have gotten there without help, but the only fingerprints to be found were Claudia's, added post mortem. It was so odd an end that when the rumors of her death were confirmed, the question remained as to whether the mask of tragedy or the mask of comedy would be more in keeping with the unfortunate end of Claudia.

CHAPTER 6

"Remember: one man's ceiling
is another man's floor."
Paul Simon

On the day of her death, it took a while to notice that Claudia was gone, and a while longer to locate her. Claudia was never the promptest of employees, and her absence from her desk went unremarked, except by Dessie, who displayed no more exasperation than usual. The people arriving for work did not tread upon her, for they entered the building by a side door open only to employees. The revolving doors in the lobby were kept locked until the box office opened at midday. On that particular day, the janitor had chosen a circuitous route to the lobby by way of a cot in one of the dressing rooms, where he'd slept for most of the morning. Moments before the first ticket buyer would arrive, his push broom in hand, he found her.

When the police arrived, the staff had already been ushered to the sidewalk, once again through the side entrance. If there were any evidence to be found on that side of the building, they trampled it once with their coming, once with their going, and once more, for good measure, when they were allowed to re-enter the building an hour later. When they finally returned to their desks, the talk was all of Claudia.

While commander-in-chief Alex huddled in her office with police officials, the lobby was closed to further traffic. The most eager members of the People's army tried to sneak downstairs to take pictures of the body, but they were sent back to their cubicles, their phones threatened with confiscation as the doors to the lobby were sealed shut. The folks at home or at TMZ would have to wait to gawk at poor Claudia. The insults following her injury hadn't ended with her death. But not everyone was giving their texting skills a workout. When Erica walked by, Zack, Zeke, and Christy were engaged in a group hug that would not quit, with the sound of muffled sobs coming from at least one member of the intertwined trio.

Upstairs, Dessie sat at her desk, clearly devastated, although her emotions did not resemble grief or any of its neighbors. She had passed most of her days shooting looks at Claudia that alternated between pity and poison, but today, she leaned forward with her head in her hands, silent. When Erica tried to console her, Dessie briefly looked up and waved her away. Erica retreated to her office, but after another forty-five minutes, she tried again, and this time, she had to insist.

"Dessie, I'm so sorry. We're not going to get any work done today, but is there anything I can do for you?"

"If you want to do something for me, leave me alone. *Please.*"

"I can't just leave you," Erica said. "There must be something . . ."

Dessie shot out her short arm and pointed in the direction of Claudia's desk.

"Will you take whatever's on her desk and deal with it? I can't look at it. Please, take it and *go.*"

Erica swept up the remains of Claudia's presence at the People's Theater, a gesture she'd repeat twice before all of the clutter from the desk had been removed. The papers and folders were heavier than they looked. As she bent over the desk for the final scoop, she noticed Claudia's oversize purse, a plain black shoulder bag, large enough to hold all her earthly possessions, spilling out of the bottom right drawer. Claudia's day must have ended in a hurry if she'd left her purse behind. Erica assumed that the police would search it soon enough, so she said nothing to Dessie, and returned to her office to sort through Claudia's inventory.

Having left her door slightly ajar, Erica tried to make sense of the debris. In retrieving it, she'd tried to be as careful as possible, but she could do little more than smooth the crumpled pages and sort them into piles that fell generally into the category of memos and correspondence. A sharper edge had dug into her arm as she lifted one of the piles, and now Erica knew why. Beneath it lay Claudia's marble notebook, the one in which she feverishly scribbled.

Well, Dessie *had* asked her to go through Claudia's papers. And it was clear to Erica that this day was, as they say, a goner. With Claudia's privacy having been violated in any number of ways, one more would hardly make a difference.

Slowly, carefully, she opened Claudia's notebook. Beginning on page one and continuing for several more was a single statement written in a childish scrawl, again and again:

I HATE THAT BITCH.

Anyone we know? Erica wondered.

It was no "All work and no play makes Jack a dull boy," but it got the point across. For page after page and line after line, this was her thesis, repeated *ad nauseum*. It was merely a warm-up to the more detailed discussion of the many flaws to be found in the woman she detested. And it quickly became clear that the woman Claudia was writing about was her mother.

Dessie should be relieved, thought Erica.

In her notebook, Claudia covered three basic topics. How she had been abandoned by her mother. How her mother had chosen her job over her child. How Claudia planned to get even with her. With an unexpected dash of drama, she called it her revenge.

Erica assumed that Claudia's mother has been forced, or perhaps even chose, to work outside the home, and, as a result, Claudia felt neglected. Many mothers had to find work in order to provide those little extras for their children, like food, clothing, shelter, and possibly college tuition. This was not unusual, nor was Claudia's reaction to it. Many children would have preferred to have mommy at home, baking cookies, just as mothers did on the reruns of those ancient television shows they watched after school, set in a time that never was. What was surprising was the anger that Claudia's notebook revealed. As far as Erica knew, Claudia had no strong feelings about anything, at least not during work hours. Unlike the bright young things that surrounded her, she seemed to have no particular attachment to a life in the theater, nor any aptitude for it. Even more surprising was the fact that Claudia had never gotten past what sounded like an adolescent rebellion. She had looked to be in her twenties, yet her ranting sounded more like someone stuck at the emotional age of fifteen, a very angry fifteen, and one that was riskily immature. Based on her writing, any harm Claudia was doing was more to herself than to others.

After her opening remarks, Claudia took an unexpected turn. Her next topic was how the people who had raised her were, as she put it, idiots. But these people did not seem to be the same ones, or at least not the same mother, who had been excoriated in the first section of her journal. These people were fools, and worse than that, they were always at home. The father worked on the family farm. The mother worked in the family kitchen, presumably baking the family cookies. As Claudia wrote,

"They were always, always, always there. Pretending to care about me. To love me. When they were really slave owners."

Slave owners? Claudia had kept the language clean, but it was good to know that you don't have to use obscenity to sound obscene. Even for Claudia, this was hyperbole. It might have been an isolating and, possibly, claustrophobic existence, but hardly illegal. Certainly not criminal.

Fascinated, Erica read on.

"That stupid girl who had me," Claudia wrote. "A local girl. So it was like I was theirs. One of them. That stupid girl. She did not give me up—she sold me. They bought me. Like a piece of livestock. On that godforsaken farm. So she could go back to living her life. She sold me and she went away."

Finally, Erica got it. Claudia had been adopted. Privately adopted, it seemed, with some form of financial incentive for the birth mother. Compensation was not unheard of, but this sounded like more than medical expenses. If this were true, Claudia might be right; she had been bought and sold. The outlines of Norman Rockwell were quickly turning into American Gothic gone bad.

Before adoption turned into a cottage industry, private adoptions were one route for would-be parents with a little bit of clout and a lot more cash. In recent years, a few states had functioned as drive-thru's for celebrities in search of their own bundle of joy. Erica, like everyone else, had seen the pictures of smiling, often single, mothers, with the new addition to the family. The rules had been tightened, but Claudia's adoption would predate all of that. Twenty or so years before, a private adoption between consenting adults could certainly have taken place. But it was the financial incentive that got Erica's attention. And it had inspired the wrath of Claudia, who was angry that she had been given up for adoption but enraged that her adoptive family had paid for the privilege of calling her their own.

For her adoptive parents, Claudia had, at best, disdain and, at worst, contempt. For her birth mother, she unbridled her anger. A woman of simple statements, Claudia made it clear what she intended for dear old mom.

"I will find her and I will kill her," Claudia wrote, again and again. "I will find her and I will kill her."

Now Claudia was dead. Did Mom find her first?

CHAPTER 7

"All I am I owe to my mother. I attribute all my success in life to
the moral, intellectual and physical education I received from her."
George Washington

"And how was your day?" Alan asked, as Erica
staggered through the door.

"You don't know?"

"I do, actually. The news was everywhere this
afternoon. I tried to call, but it was impossible to get
through. How are you?"

Erica's ashen face made any answer redundant.

"Nothing I could say would do justice to it," she
began.

"That's a start," Alan said.

"Someone killed Dessie's assistant, Claudia," Erica
said. "In a building full of people who want your
attention, someone killed the one person who tried to be
invisible. Why would someone do that?"

"Beats me," said Alan, drawing her out by saying as
little as possible.

"I don't get it," said Erica. "It was horrible,
humiliating."

"For you?"

"No," said Erica, shaking off the suggestion. "For
her. She had been posed in a corner of the lobby. To
look like a figure from Michelangelo's *The Creation of
Man.*

"She played God?"

"Someone did. But, no—she was Adam."

"At this performance, the role of Adam, usually played by—"

"Nowhere near funny, Alan."

"I'm sorry," he said, a little sheepishly.

"And this is the show that no one's supposed to talk about—"

"Now they will," said Alan.

"And, oh, by the way," Erica added, "I saw the mock up of the poster art. They're using a modified version of *The Creation of Man* as the model. Similar enough to the original to be recognizable, but not quite enough to get sued."

"An odd coincidence," said Alan.

"I can't imagine this is someone's idea of a publicity stunt," Erica continued. "That's too sick for words." She paused, before saying,

"Alan, if you want to make me feel better, why don't you pour us a glass of wine. Or two or three. Although I don't think there's enough wine in France—"

"Well, we can give it a try," he said, moving toward the refrigerator. "How is Dessie taking all this?"

"I would describe her as shaken but not stirred."

"What's that supposed to mean?" Alan wanted to know, as he uncorked the medicinal bottle of white wine that could always be found in the refrigerator.

"She was upset. In shock, I guess," Erica said. "But very, very quiet. No tears that I saw."

"You said they didn't really get along. From what you've told me, Dessie was pretty much carrying her in this job. And from what I know of Dessie, she's not the type for histrionics. She'd save it for the stage. Or skip it altogether."

"No, it's not that," Erica insisted. "I didn't expect Dessie to make a show of her emotions. That's not her style. But she didn't seem to be feeling anything. She just put her head down and wanted the world to go away."

"The world included you?"

"Yes, strange as that may seem. Garbo wanted to be alone. She did ask me to clear off the top of Claudia's desk. And then, get out. So I did as she asked, then I went to my office and stayed there until they sent us all home for the day."

For the time being, Erica chose to keep Claudia's literary efforts to herself.

"The police didn't want to go through everything in or on Claudia's desk?" asked Alan.

"I didn't think of that," Erica admitted. "I assume they took whatever interested them. I did notice that Claudia's purse—more like a sack—was still in the bottom drawer of her desk. In any case, at the People's Theater, we play by Dessie's rules. Refuse her at your peril. So if Dessie says to clean off the top of Claudia's desk—"

"You do," said Alan.

"That is correct, sir," Erica replied. "Besides, the papers were pretty routine. I'll run it by Dessie in the morning to see if there's anything that needs to go to the authorities."

Before she perused it, Erica had assumed that Claudia's marble notebook would contain the innocuous ramblings of a frequent scribbler and that Dessie would have made the same assumption if she had noticed that the notebook was still on the desk.

"Yes, I'll ask Dessie about it tomorrow," Erica repeated, as she collected her thoughts, then said, "A murder at the People's Theater—"

"I heard that she died—" Alan started to say.

"Yes, it was a Kemby award," Erica confirmed. "Bad news certainly travels fast. And we both know *how* it travels fast. The last thing I heard from the hordes of eager newshounds—otherwise known as the kids with texting capabilities, which is all of them—is that someone smacked her upside, well, backside the head. Then the Kemby was placed in Claudia's hand, with her fingers curled around it. So, to paraphrase Charlton Heston, someone most of these kids probably never heard of—"

"They had to pry the Kemby from her cold, dead hands?" Alan offered.

"One hand, to be perfectly accurate," said Erica, before she was caught by another thought.

"You didn't tell Dessie about the business at Brixton, did you?" asked Erica.

"Of course not. Proximity to murder isn't exactly a resume builder," Alan answered.

"Not as a rule," Erica agreed. "Dessie never said anything, but I just wondered." She shook her head as she continued, "Oh, you should have seen Dessie, Alan. She was in an awful state today."

"With the notable exception of you, Erica, how often do you think people deal with this sort of thing?"

"Yes, I see your point. Dessie just strikes me as someone who is calm in a crisis. I bet she's had plenty of practice in her own life," Erica said.

"Yes, but this isn't your standard-issue, single-working-mother kind of stuff," Alan replied.

"True," Erica agreed. "And she revived enough at the end of the day to show me a back exit out of the theater. We managed to avoid most of the cameras. The lobby was locked for obvious reasons, so all the bright young things were making a beeline for the side entrance and into the loving arms of the reporters on the sidewalk."

"Yes," said Alan, "I saw them on the early news. They all knew Claudia, they all loved her—"

"And most of them would have difficulty picking her out of a lineup."

"Looking for their moment of fame," he began.

"But they didn't know her, Alan. Maybe she encouraged that. And if they did know her, they tolerated her at best."

"Did you? What was she like?" he asked.

"Hard to say," she answered. "And hard to know. For the most part, Claudia hid behind her hair. But occasionally you might catch a glimpse of an expression. From what little I could see, she went through life looking like a calf that just found out where veal comes from."

"Where did she come from?" Alan wanted to know.

"A planet far, far away," Erica replied. "I don't know. Maine, maybe? I think that's what Dessie said. Claudia was not one of the crowd. They were going places. She was sitting still. Very still."

"Then why was she there?" asked Alan.

"Damned if I know," Erica answered.

"But you're going to stay out of it," ventured Alan.

"I just got here," said Erica. "I have no attachment to the victim or to the venue, for that matter. I promise to sit at my desk and shuffle my papers. If asked, I'll answer questions to the best of my limited ability."

"Are they starting to interview the staff yet?"

"Slowly but surely," said Erica. "So far, everyone gets the same questions. Did you know her? Did she have any enemies? Where were you on the night in question? The truthful answers go something like this: which one was she again? I sat over here. She sat over there. Never the twain met."

"What never?" asked Alan.

"Hardly ever," said Erica.

"Okay, good," said Alan. "So you'll lay low on this one."

"Yes," Erica promised. "And speaking of laying."

"I'm way ahead of you—" he said.

"Bring the wine," she said.

CHAPTER 8

*"Merry and tragical? Tedious and brief?
That is hot ice and wondrous strange snow."*
William Shakespeare, *A Midsummer Night's Dream*

"MONA LISA FROWN" screamed the tabloid of record from the corner newsstand, as a slightly hung over Erica made her way to work the next morning. Someone had unearthed a photo of Claudia that looked as bleary as Erica felt. Claudia certainly did not look happy, but given the circumstances, who would? *And they got the artist wrong,* thought Erica. *DaVinci again! Stealing what should be Michelangelo's thunder.*

Upon arriving at work, Erica headed straight for Dessie's desk, avoiding the crowds of thrill seekers and professional ghouls milling on the sidewalk. Dessie was nowhere to be seen, but Alex's door was open for the first time since Claudia's untimely passing, and a conversation was in progress.

"Do you think they have any . . . suspects?" Erica heard Dessie ask.

"No, not yet," Alex replied. "They think it was a crime of passion, given that she was killed with more force than was needed." Alex paused. "They say that a more experienced killer wouldn't have been so . . . elaborate," she continued. "A professional would just do the job and be done with it. But the whole staging business." There was a catch in her voice as she said it. "A professional wouldn't call attention to himself. Or herself," she said.

Hooray for our side, thought Erica. *Women are now included in the pool of potential killers.*

Alex went on. "Given that the body was in a state of *rigor mortis* when it was found, the police are putting the time of death between 8 and 11 on Monday night. And there's something called 'lividity,' which means the body becomes discolored when the heart stops beating. They can tell if the body was moved or repositioned based upon where the blood settles. Her body had been moved."

"Moved? How?" asked Dessie.

"A rolling desk chair. They found it in a closet nearby. Where they keep the supplies for the concession stand. Napkins and cups and that sort of thing. Some of Claudia's hair was snagged on the chair along with traces of . . . "

Alex could not bring herself to continue. Dessie stepped in, as she always did.

"Yes, I heard. The same as they found on the Kemby," Dessie said. "And no prints?" she continued.

"None," said Alex. "And no defensive wounds on Claudia, which means she didn't fight back. So someone came prepared. That's what the police find so baffling. It looks amateurish, but also planned. A crime of passion but cold at the same time. Definitely overkill."

"Do they think she knew her assailant?" Dessie asked.

"They didn't say," Alex answered.

"Do they have any idea why she was posed that way?" Dessie inquired.

"No," answered Alex, more firmly this time. "The police think we should know. It's the same picture as the poster for *Michelangelo.* It's our show."

Claudia didn't strike that pose on her own, thought Erica. *And someone has a strange sense of humor.*

"No fingerprints at all?" asked Dessie.

"None that mean anything," replied Alex. "Even with a cleaning crew, let's imagine how many sets of prints you can find in a theater lobby."

"The theater was dark that night," said Dessie. "No performances, not even any rehearsals—"

"Which almost never happens around here," said Alex. "It seems there was no one left in the theater. What time did you leave?" she asked.

"The usual time," said Dessie. "I had to get home to the kids."

"Was anyone else around?" asked Alex.

"Not that I saw," Dessie answered.

"Then you may have been the last person to see her alive," said Alex, with a tone of wonder in her voice.

"The last but one," answered Dessie, sounding less awestruck.

"Did you notice anything odd about her behavior that day?"

"Alex, there was always something odd about her behavior."

"Come on, Dessie, the girl is dead."

"That's the way it was, Alex," Dessie insisted. "Claudia kept to herself. She did her work, more or less. She went home. I didn't know much more about her. Do you?"

"You worked with her every day," countered Alex. "I just walked by her."

"You hired her," said Dessie.

"Well, that letter got her in the door," Alex admitted. "I liked her initiative. You know as well as I do that you don't get from where she started to here without some help or a huge amount of determination."

"Which one did you have, Alex?"

"The latter, as you well know," she replied.

"That New England resolve," Dessie agreed.

"Which we both know something about," said Alex. "But this is not about me or you," she added. "After Claudia was hired, it was up to her to do something with the opportunity she was given. And apparently, she didn't."

"Not so you'd notice," Dessie said carefully.

"But this—how could this happen?" Alex continued. "To kill her and then to leave her like that. It's sick and it's cruel. And it couldn't come at a worse time. We don't want anything to harm the Michelangelo project."

"It won't," said Dessie. "Face it, Alex, the word was already out on *Michelangelo*. Now the gossip mill is working overtime. People are calling about tickets to a show that hasn't been cast yet."

"You know what's at stake, Dessie. We can't allow anything to damage the People's Theater or its reputation."

"I *know*," Dessie said. "And it won't."

As she listened, Erica couldn't help but notice how quickly Claudia had been dropped from the conversation. Her death was a terrible thing, to be sure, but the play was always the thing. And as far as its two chief caregivers were concerned, all that really mattered was the continued survival of the People's Theater. Come what may, they appeared to be united in that effort, for different, if intersecting, reasons.

"Can I help you?"

Erica turned to the voice behind her, as Ron Vartan looked quizzically at her. She calculated how long he'd been standing there, and decided that he wouldn't have been able to contain himself if he'd caught her eavesdropping outside Alex's door. Ron must have watched her for only a moment before interrupting her stakeout.

Erica smiled at him, through slightly gritted teeth. "I should be asking the same question," she said. "What can I do for you, Ron?"

"I need to see Alex," he said with apparent irritation. "She asked me to research an alarm system for the awards case."

After several decades of leaving the trophies in an unlocked case, Erica thought, *the next step might be laser beams and flashing lights, particularly if Ron had his way.* But she offered no opinion and stepped aside, pointing to Alex's open door.

"Then, in you should go. I think Dessie's with her."

Ron huffed his displeasure as he passed by her to enter. As he did, he nearly bumped into Dessie, who was making her own hasty exit.

"Ron. Always a pleasure," said Dessie as she narrowly avoided him, saved only by her size and her agility.

"Dessie," was all that Ron could muster.

Seeing Erica standing there, Dessie asked the question of the day: "Erica, what can I do for you?" In the course of a little more than twelve hours, Dessie's tone had returned to normal, and, other than a brow that was slightly more furrowed than usual, so had she.

"I'm glad to see you're feeling better after yesterday," Erica said.

"I'm fine," Dessie insisted. "Life goes on."

"For some of us, anyway," Erica replied, before moving to the next topic. "I wanted you to know that I went through the papers on Claudia's desk. There was nothing special. I put it all in a couple of folders."

"Leave them on my desk when you get a chance," said Dessie, moving in the direction of the piles of paper on her own desk.

"Sure," said Erica. "Oh, and there was one more thing. Under the papers was that notebook Claudia used to write in. I looked through it. Let's just say, she had some unresolved issues toward her parents, her mother especially. It probably has nothing to do with anything, but I wondered if it should be turned over to the police. You know, just to complete the picture of Claudia. The Claudia we never knew."

This bit of news appeared to get Dessie's attention. "Really," she said. "Well, give it to me, and I'll pass it along. You never know what the police might find interesting."

"Will do," said Erica.

"You know, I'll take those papers now," added Dessie, following Erica to her office. "No time like the present."

As Erica walked by Claudia's now empty desk, she noticed that the large black purse was no longer spilling out of Claudia's now empty bottom drawer. She assumed that the police had taken it as some form of evidence. Evidence of what, it was harder to say.

"Here you go," said Erica, passing Dessie the two file folders filled with slightly crumpled pages. Dessie took the folders, placed them under her arm, and stood waiting.

"Oh, the notebook," Erica said. She leaned over and pulled it out of her own desk drawer in which she had recently stowed it. "Here you go again," she said, as she handed the book to Dessie.

"Fine, then," said Dessie, as she turned to walk away. "I'm sure you have something to keep you busy."

"Always," replied Erica. "Oh, by the way, Dessie?"

"Yes?" she asked, her voice rising.

"Will there be some kind of memorial service for Claudia? I mean, here at the theater?"

The People's Theater was no stranger to memorial services. The AIDS epidemic had cut a swath through the People's people, as it had through the theater at large. Back in the eighties, and for about a decade thereafter, many staff members could not bear another Friday afternoon spent counting their losses, however deeply they grieved for the departed. But Claudia was another case entirely.

"Actually, no," said Dessie. "I'm sure it would be standing room only, but an uncle and aunt, her closest living relatives, have asked that, given the circumstances of her death, there be no public memorial. At least, not here. The medical examiner has released the body, and she will be shipped back home, to Maine. Maybe the news coverage is more discreet there, and they can bury her in peace. I wish them luck," said Dessie.

"That's too bad," said Erica. "A service could provide some form of closure," she added. "Even if people didn't know her all that well."

"They'll have to get by with Alex providing updates on the case as they become available," said Dessie. "She feels that people should be informed."

"Well, it won't give them the warm fuzzies, but if it's all they have," said Erica.

"It is," said Dessie. "Trust me."

The short-lived plan for interoffice updates was discontinued once it became clear that the information being offered was already available on the news or online. It had become common knowledge that the murder weapon offered no prints other than Claudia's. Rumor had it that the awards case offered more than its share of fingerprints, including Claudia's, Alex's, Dessie's, and most of the cleaning crew. Good to know the cleaners were on the job, leaving prints if not wiping them off. While visiting Alex's office, a number of dignitaries had touched the case, if not the Kemby, with more than a few looking longingly in its direction.

For these important personages, names were taken but not prints: that would be saved for a much later date.

The terrible and the wonderful thing about a complex as vast as the People's Theater is that there are so many opportunities for concealment. Although the building was allegedly empty on the night that Claudia died, someone had placed the body in a corner of the lobby, not the most public of places, but compared with the far flung corners that were available, it was openly on display. This might have been the result of haste on the part of the murderer, but there was always the elevator and the cover of darkness to aid and abet transport to a quieter corner, or so the staff had decided in numerous discussions on the subject. Within a few weeks, even these debates died down, and life at the People's Theater returned to a form of normal. People were more interested in the progress of *Michelangelo: The Musical*. Instead of the details of Claudia's death, these were the tidbits that were savored.

CHAPTER 9

"In the room the women come and go,
Talking of Michelangelo."
T. S. Eliot, "The Love Song of J. Alfred Prufrock"

The death of Claudia was a blow, but as everyone at the People's Theater knew, the show must go on . . . and they were sure that Claudia would have wanted it that way. So, casting continued apace. A very wide net pulled in more than the usual suspects. The word was that *Michelangelo: The Musical* had the potential to be a hit on the scale of *The Brothers Wittgenstein*. In the theater, hope springs eternal.

Erica watched the notables troop in and out of Alex's office. Talent was all well and good, but name recognition was what got people into the seats. One such contender was an actress who had toiled on Off- and Off-Off-Broadway stages until she had the audition that changed everything: the television pilot that turned into a series that turned into a hit. She played the mom, the only woman in a houseful of clueless men, in a show created for a male audience, ages 18-49. It was a sure-fire formula—testosterone with a laugh track—and according to the wisdom of television programming, if it works once, it will work every time.

With the financial rewards of one hit TV show, an actor can return to the theater at regular intervals—even Off-Broadway—and still live the very good life. Eight years later, the actress had no financial need to work. And now that she was a name, she was offered a part she would never have read for in her stage-acting prime. The audience already felt comfortable with her; after all, they let her into their home once a week. Why wouldn't they want to see her live and in person?

In truth, she had returned to New York for a little career recovery. The series may have done wonders for her bank account, but after a few seasons, she could almost set her watch by the time in the script when she would deliver her one laugh line and retreat to the kitchen. A profound case of boredom had set in. Wisely, she decided to fill her time with a new set of interests, but there is only so much yoga a person can do. Unwisely, she began to date one of her co-stars. Not the man who played her husband or the one who played the wacky neighbor. No, she zeroed in on the actor who played her son. Her youngest son. In the grand tradition of sitcoms that employ actors playing teenagers, the average age of those still roaming the halls of the local high school was twenty four. The actor in question was eighteen; he was legal, but just barely. And she was, in fact, old enough to be his mother. His own mother was unavailable for comment due to the fact that the young man had asked the court to declare him an emancipated minor at the age of fourteen, relieving his mother of her managerial duties. At the time, she relinquished her maternal ones as well.

After a few dates in semi-public places that couldn't be explained away as publicity for the show, their association, although short-lived, became public knowledge. In hindsight, it might have been smarter to insist that she was advising him on where to apply to college. The fact that the young man had never graduated from high school might have hampered that explanation, but it beat their non-denial denial that anything was going on. And the alleged affair didn't harm the show's prospects. The sitcom was breathing its last before heading to syndication heaven, the sudden notoriety spurring audience interest in the endless reruns ahead. Now, people could look for, but not find, hints of a more-than-maternal interest by a mother in her son. The minor scandal hadn't hurt the actress's prospects either, the older woman as "cougar" being in season. Granted, she stood right on the edge of career-ending, if not criminal, behavior, but she, like her young friend, had escaped essentially unscathed, their reputations curiously enhanced.

So, she came to New York looking for a hit. Fearing that Broadway might hit back, she chose to bide her time Off-Broadway until something better came along. Then, something better did come along. Of course, she would be playing someone's mother, but this was nothing new. Michelangelo had a very young mother. And instead of facing the twilight of her career, as it would be for so many actresses of a certain age—that age being twenty five in Hollywood, thirty five in New York—she was looking at a hit, a palpable hit, or so everyone said.

"And I hear they got Miranda Owen for Mike's mom," Erica said to Dessie, as they made their way back from the copy room, their arms full of documents too sensitive for the inquiring eyes of the younger members of the People's army.

"Yes, lucky us," said Dessie, with a distinct lack of enthusiasm.

"Do you know her?" asked Erica.

"Only a little," Dessie answered. "Martin knew her. They dated for a while."

"Oh," said Erica, a little surprised at Dessie's reaction, given how much time must have passed since then. "What did he say about her?"

"Not much," said Dessie. "She was one of many, long before he met me." Dessie readjusted the pile of papers she was carrying to even the load. "It's pretty clear her tastes have changed over the years. From what I hear, she's probably scouring Facebook for her next conquest."

"Tindr's more like it," said Erica. "How old was Martin when he knew her?"

"I'm pretty sure he could vote," said Dessie.

"Well, she's gonna love this place. The average age among the male population looks to be at the lower end of twenty."

"And some of them are even straight," said Dessie.

"All the better," Erica agreed. "But speaking of Mike's mom, she died before he was six. According to some historians, he barely knew his mother, the lovely Francesca, because he was shipped off to a wet nurse/nanny when he was about a month old. It did not inspire warm family feelings. And although his dad, Ludovico, came from a prominent Florentine family, any claim to noble birth was fading fast. With Ludovico too proud to hold down a job, well, it wasn't a pretty family picture. Later in life, Mike had to bail out his dad—financially, that is—on a regular basis. The only family member he was close to was a younger brother, Buonarroto. They stayed in touch."

"I'm so glad we put you on the case," said Dessie, smiling. "I know just who to ask when I need a fun fact from the life and times of Michelangelo."

"In fact," Erica continued, "the Sistine Chapel, one of Mike's greatest hits, was named for Pope Sixtus IV, who had it built—"

"Sixtus, Sistine, I get it," said Dessie.

"And it was decorated by his nephew, Pope Julius II," finished Erica.

"There's always a nephew who does the decorating," Dessie added.

"Our Mike managed to cover 12,000 square feet of Sistine ceiling between 1508 and 1512. Strangely enough, he didn't want the commission at first, thinking it only served to inflate the ego of a pope who was hardly an unfettered man of the cloth."

"Do tell," said Dessie.

"Sixtus also signed off on the Spanish Inquisition," said Erica, "but then he wasn't too happy with the abuse of power that resulted."

"Well, no one expects the Spanish Inquisition," Dessie replied. "By the way, is there an *off* button I can push right about now?" she asked.

"I'm done," said Erica.

"Not that we don't appreciate your enthusiasm for the project," said Dessie, "but we should probably stick to our version of events for the time being."

"Fine with me," said Erica.

"Yes, Mike's mom does die in the first act," Dessie continued. "But the script pretends that they actually knew each other. And even liked each other. More importantly, she gets a song before she goes. In fact, you should expect a giant sob-fest before intermission."

"I'll have my hanky ready."

"I was out of the office when Miranda came in to talk to Alex," Dessie continued, "but I hear she's really skinny. Television skinny. *Scary* television skinny. Just who I'd pick for an Italian matron with pretensions of grandeur. In those days, you kept some meat on your bones to show that you weren't poor."

"Maybe she'll gain some weight for the part," Erica said.

Dessie quickly dismissed that suggestion. "Not since DeNiro in *Raging Bull*. We were all impressed by that performance, but from then on, it was a fat suit and prosthetics. Or we ignore the actor's appearance and cast for name recognition."

"Yes," said Erica, "I'm becoming familiar with the 'butts-in-the-seats' theory and how we get them there."

She thought for a moment. "It's just too bad," she said. "There are probably a thousand talented actresses in the tri-state area alone, all of whom look the part and can act it and won't get a chance to read for it."

"It's true, Erica. On the plus side, the People's Theater is known for giving the unknowns a chance—someone like Alan, for example. But this time, they're not messing around. It's a big-budget production, by our standards. We need butts in the seats at all costs. Now, we're not going to embarrass ourselves with stunt casting that will come back and bite us—"

"In the butt?" said Erica helpfully.

"Or anywhere else," finished Dessie. "We want to make sure the audience gets to the theater, and Miss Miranda sells tickets. The cast won't all be television names and faces," Dessie continued. "I'm sure she'll be fine, by the way. Once upon a time, she was on that short list of talented people who could play the hell out of the part and never got the chance. And if she's not fine, then trust me, she's out."

"I always do," said Erica. "I always do."

"That's what we like to hear," said Dessie. "Now, will you do me a favor? Stop by Ron's office and ask him to come in to see me. My phone has been behaving strangely all day, and I don't feel like yelling across the floor at him."

"Okay, Dessie," said Erica.

"To sweeten the deal, I'll even carry your half of the papers," Dessie added.

"Can you handle all of this?" asked Erica. "It's really not necessary—"

"Not a problem," said Dessie. "Tell him fifteen minutes."

"Okay," said Erica.

"And I have an errand for you this afternoon," continued Dessie. "I'll give you the details once I finish with Ron."

Erica had never seen the inside of Ron's office, having no reason, as well as no desire, to go there. Ron usually made his presence felt outside Alex's office, so Erica saw his back as he passed her office on the way to the inner sanctum.

His own inner sanctum was a humbler affair, a cubicle with high walls and no ceiling. The better to hear you, my dear, as the army of the ambitious had come to learn. He did not have spies everywhere because he didn't need them: the sound bouncing off a tin roof made private conversations a virtual impossibility. That's where texting came in, and they were adept at tap-tap-tapping their days away, thus avoiding his prying ears.

Ron spent a part of his day tap-tap-tapping on his computer, creating budgets, reports, and other documents that made him feel important. When Erica stopped at the opening of his cubicle, she was surprised to see two things: One, the room was immaculate, not a paper out of place or in sight. The file folders in a stand on his desk were lined up evenly, with their flaps carefully aligned so that one tab did not block the next. And two, he wore clear vinyl gloves while he typed, the kind that people use to protect their hands from harmful chemicals when gardening, cleaning, or pursuing a hobby that might damage a manicure. Ron seemed to be doing none of the above.

"Yes?" he asked as he looked away from the computer screen and saw Erica.

"Um, Dessie asked me to ask you to stop by in fifteen minutes for a meeting. She didn't call because she's having a problem with her phone—"

"Why are you delivering her messages?" Ron began. "Why didn't she send Claud—"

About halfway through the name, it was clear that Ron had realized his mistake.

"Tell Dessie I'll be there," he said brusquely.

"Sure thing," said Erica, turning on her heel and leaving.

Erica quickly crossed the floor to return to her office, after pausing briefly outside Dessie's to confirm that her task had been completed. Apparently, Dessie's phone was working again, for she was engaged in a call, seemingly to one of her children.

"I said we will make the cupcakes when I get home. No, you cannot begin until I get there. Maude knows that. We will talk about this later. I *said* when I get home."

Dessie looked up and saw Erica standing at the door.

"New sitter," she said, holding her hand over the receiver. "The kids are testing her."

"How's she doing?" asked Erica.

"For the time being, we're keeping it pass/fail," said Dessie, before returning to the phone conversation. "No. I said *no*. I have to get back to work now. We'll talk about this when I get home."

"Good to see that your phone's working again," said Erica, as she returned to her own office. "Ron will be over in 15."

Dessie nodded but made no reply.

A little later that afternoon, Dessie appeared at Erica's door. In one hand, she gripped a set of keys with a distinctive key chain. In the other she held the black strap of Claudia's shoulder bag that she dragged across the floor.

"Interesting key chain," said Erica. "Is that Nemo?"

"As in *Finding Nemo*. Yes," said Dessie. "It's Claudia's. They're her keys."

"I recognize the bag," said Erica. "Wasn't Claudia a little old for a cartoon-character key chain?"

"I'd say it was kitsch, but I know full well it wasn't," said Dessie, looking at the slightly dilapidated fish. "I think she was a true believer. It must have meant something to her."

"Isn't Nemo the one who wants to find his way home . . . to his parents?" asked Erica.

"Parent," said Dessie. "Mom doesn't make it out of the first reel. My kids watched that movie endlessly," she said, "but even they are too old for it now."

"Claudia wasn't," said Erica, adding, "I assume Nemo made it."

"Happy ending all around," said Dessie.

"Go, Nemo," said Erica. *Though not such a happy ending for Claudia*, she remembered, before inquiring, "What's the errand?"

Well, here it is," said Dessie. "Claudia's next of kin are emptying her apartment and taking her stuff back to Maine. *They're* not doing it—they hired a moving company, so they don't have to leave the farm. The trip to pick up her remains was all that they could manage. I guess the cows and the chickens would miss them too much. Or maybe they grow potatoes? I don't know. Anyway, they have no interest in coming back to the big city, and they refuse to set foot here. Alex offered to meet with them, but they weren't having any of it. But they did ask that her possessions, the things she left here, be packed up and sent to them."

"The police are finished with her bag?" Erica asked.

Dessie hesitated for a moment before answering. "It's here, not in a locked room at the local precinct, so I'm guessing it's not chock full of evidence. The thing is, this task will take more than a trip to UPS."

"Okay," said Erica, stretching out the word.

"The family—the aunt and uncle—I think they blame us—the theater—for Claudia's death."

"Do they have a particular suspect in mind?" asked Erica.

"No, they don't. But their thinking is, apparently, she came to work here and she died. By their logic, if she hadn't come to work here, she'd still be alive."

"Interesting logic," said Erica. "And, obviously, it wasn't a mugging."

"No, her purse and wallet are still here," echoed Dessie.

"And I'd rule out a random act of violence," Erica continued. "Someone had to know his or her way to that awards cabinet—it's not something you stumble on," she said.

"No, it's not," said Dessie, sounding a little annoyed. "But my job is not to solve this thing. I'm just trying to do what I can to honor the family's request. I want us to be done with this, at least as far as the People's Theater is concerned."

"Well, the media's certainly helping you out. They dropped poor Claudia like a hot potato," said Erica.

"Not a lot to say about her," said Dessie.

"Other than she was murdered," Erica countered.

"I guess they said that, sold a few papers, and moved on," said Dessie. "So should we. So *must* we," she added.

"I'm ready if you are," answered Erica. "What do you want me to do?"

"Sending the family this bag should take care of it," said Dessie. "And there's one more thing."

"Yes?"

"I'm sorry to put this on you, but you are one of our few employees with the maturity and the tact. And I'm pretty sure you don't know how to send pictures on your phone."

"How did you guess?"

"Good. So, I think I can trust you not to exploit the situation and share what you find with the world. What the family asks is that someone—that would be you—go to Claudia's apartment and pick out anything that looks like it's of value—sentimental, financial, whatever—and stick it in the bag, which we will then send to them."

"That would be me?" said Erica. "These people have no use for us—not that I entirely blame them—but they trust us—me?—to go through their niece's stuff and send them anything that looks interesting?"

"Erica, think about it. It's pretty unlikely that Claudia has anything of value—they know that. They just prefer to have us do the looking rather than having the movers do it. You don't have to dig too deeply. Just take a quick look around."

"I don't suppose you'd like to join me?" asked Erica.

"I don't really see this as a two-person job," answered Dessie.

"But I didn't really know her," said Erica.

"Another plus," said Dessie. "Not knowing Claudia might make your visit a little easier."

"So you want me to bring my keen eye to the task?"

"I want you to bring your objective eye," said Dessie.

"Should I bring my jeweler's eye?" asked Erica.

"I don't think that will be necessary. I doubt you're going to trip over her collection of fine gems," Dessie replied.

"When do you want me to go?"

"How about now?" Dessie said as she held out a crumpled piece of paper. "Here's the mailing address in Maine. After you're finished at the apartment, you can hit the UPS office. Send whatever you find at their super-speedy rate. Keep the receipt and we'll reimburse you. Then you're done for the day."

"Sounds like a plan," said Erica, without a trace of enthusiasm. "But a quick question before I go. What's with Ron and the gloves? Does he have allergies?"

"Do you know anyone who's allergic to a computer keyboard?" asked Dessie.

"So, he's a germ-phobe," Erica continued.

"Wrong again," said Dessie.

"I give up," said Erica.

"He puts a little aloe vera in the gloves. He can moisturize while he works at the computer, which he does for a good part of the day."

"Quite the multitasker," Erica said, impressed. "Okay, then. What's Claudia's address?"

CHAPTER 10

"Carving is easy, you just go down to the skin and stop."
Michelangelo

Claudia lived on a street in the East Thirties. If she had lived a few blocks west, it would have been a nicer address and probably beyond her means. As it was, the front of the building had a steady view of the traffic making its way to the Midtown Tunnel. The windows facing the street didn't appear to be the triple-paned kind that could block the noise of unending car horns and complaints. No, these looked like landlord specials, the kind that barely block out a gentle rain. But none of this would have been of concern to Claudia, for, as Erica discovered, her apartment was situated at the back of the building. The building had no doorman, so there was no one who required an explanation; besides, Erica had a set of keys, a clear mission, and the ability to look as though she belonged there, should anybody ask. No one did. The other tenants were at work or locked behind their doors.

The sound of a lone television was almost a comfort as Erica quickly made her way up the stairs—there was no elevator either. Her trek was a short one, for Claudia lived on the second floor. It took a little jiggling of the key on the Nemo key chain to turn the lock on the apartment door. Once the door was opened, Erica knew that her first impression of the apartment would be a lasting one.

"Cell Block C has nothing on this place," she said to no one in particular. The door opened to a long, narrow hallway, with no decoration of any kind, which led to an only slightly wider room. The main room and the only room. Clustered in the right-hand corner was a Pullman kitchen, with a stove, a sink, and a half-sized refrigerator. The stove boasted two burners instead of the traditional four, but Erica doubted that Claudia did much cooking. On the left side of the room was a round white café table with a single folding chair, so Claudia appeared to do little entertaining. A bathroom was tucked into the left-hand wall. What would probably serve as the conversation piece of the room, if there were anyone there to talk to, was a well worn sofa, which had the look of having been left by a previous tenant. Once upon a time it had been red. The sofa, which did double duty as Claudia's bed, was placed in front of the only window in the room, a double set of casements that took up most of the back wall. This could be charming—light! air!—were it not for the fact that the windows were almost completely blocked by a gate fastened with a lock that looked like it meant business. No one would be getting into or out of the apartment through this particular aperture. This was reassuring until you noticed that the fire escape was on the other side of the metal grill. In case of fire, you would have to find the keys, unlock the gate, open the window, and make your way down the fire escape, all in record time. Depending upon which way the flames were fanning, Claudia could alternatively run down the stairs and hope there wasn't a stampede. But for day-to-day living, the locked windows made for a cheerless environment that could easily induce depression in the most jovial of souls, which Claudia was not.

There had been no yellow tape crisscrossing Claudia's door, marking this as the site of someone's catastrophe, so Erica assumed that the police had come and gone, having looked into the corners of Claudia's life, and finding or not finding something that would explain what happened to her. Erica assumed it was the latter. Not far from Claudia's dining area sat a low, pock-marked bureau, probably harvested from the sidewalk on trash day, with three mostly empty drawers, their contents scattered for all to see. Tee shirts, sweaters, jeans, a few scarves and unmentionables: the sum total of Claudia's life was strewn around the apartment. Either Claudia was a disastrous housekeeper or someone had been thorough in the search.

Claudia's relatives had chosen not to make this journey, which would be painful for a number of reasons, but a quick inventory revealed that little of this merchandise would need transporting. Erica hoped that they had instructed the movers to stop short of the furniture that had outlived its usefulness, or belonged back on the sidewalk for another New York neophyte. But it was the family's choice to handle this task long distance, and if the cows ended up with a couch to lounge upon, so much the better.

Erica picked her way across the room, trying not to step on the details of Claudia's life. On the floor, barely visible, was a round, clear bead, the size of a dime. When her foot found the bead, Erica skidded, but she caught herself by leaning on an old television set with a tiny screen. Two twisted wire hangers that served as its antenna would have given Joan Crawford new reasons to exclaim against them. Claudia's entertainment center was supported by a packing box facing the sofa. When the box began to wobble, Erica quickly moved out of the way before it toppled over. Not quickly enough, for the television fell sideways, not quite crashing to the floor, but tilting precariously in the direction of the sofa, while the cardboard box tipped at an angle. In the disheveled setting, no one—the movers, in particular—would notice the difference, but Erica did not want to disrupt things any further. She carefully placed the television on the sofa before righting the box. As she did, one of the box's flaps fell open. Inside, secured by packing tape to the top of the box, was a large manila envelope. The envelope was stiff and had served as an additional brace for the television it supported. It wasn't much of a hiding place but served its purpose. No one else had noticed it, but no one else had been as clumsy as Erica in crossing the room. This was, perhaps, the key to a successful search—stumbling over the evidence missed by others.

If there had been others. Erica began to wonder about the all-clear given by Dessie. Had she arranged it with the authorities, or had she taken matters into her own hands? All publicity is good publicity, as long as they spell your name right, but whatever benefit the People's Theater might gain from a dead body discovered in their lobby had probably expired. Sympathy can be fleeting, and before compassion turned to cruelty, Dessie seemed determined to shift the focus from Claudia: The Dead Girl to *Michelangelo: The Musical*.

Erica reached into the box and carefully pulled off the packing tape, then separated the envelope from its sanctuary. She opened the envelope and pulled out its contents. Out slid a black marble notebook, a twin to the one she had already inspected.

"Oh, my God, there's a Volume Two," Erica said. Sitting down carefully on the sofa, so as not to add to a tear in the fabric, she read.

Based on the available evidence, Claudia's mind, at least as far as her writing life was concerned, followed a single theme. In Volume One, she stated in no uncertain terms that she hated her mother—her birth mother—and had limited patience for her adoptive parents. Volume Two was on the same track with a slight turn. She hated the woman who had given birth to her and then given her up. And she would find her.

Erica has seen enough. She would read more at her leisure, but now she wanted to vacate the premises as soon as possible. She needed to decide quickly what would be heading back to Maine.

What should her family remember her by? Erica could choose between a blue silk scarf with a peacock pattern, possibly a birthday gift from someone with good taste, or the endless denunciation of the birth mother who had looked out for her daughter, in her way. Erica chose the scarf, a few brass trinkets that passed as jewelry, and a green cotton shirt from a local consignment shop, the tag still on it. Apparently, Claudia liked to string beads in her spare time, designing intricate necklaces and bracelets as a break from composing the screeds that condemned her birth mother to the lower circles of hell. Erica found several bracelets and a few unfinished pieces at the back of the top drawer in the bureau, along with packets of beads in a variety of colors. Medium blue and light pink were the clear favorites in the artist's palette. Erica added these to her collection of gifts, which fit easily into the black expanse of Claudia's shoulder bag, which would fit neatly into a UPS box. Claudia's marble notebook would fit neatly into Erica's bag, and there it would stay until she decided what to do with it. It could always be mailed at a later date, an unexpected discovery from the bottomless treasure trove that was Claudia's life.

Erica hoisted Claudia's bag to her shoulder as she took a last look around the place that Claudia called home. Fingering the oddly-attired key chain, Erica gave the room a final good bye, saying, "Nemo. No one. I get it, Claudia."

She made sure the door locked after her.

CHAPTER 11

"Trust yourself. You know more than you think."
Benjamin Spock

"You did what!"

"Come on, Alan. It wasn't like I was breaking and entering. I had the keys. Plus explicit instructions from Dessie," said Erica, trying to soothe him.

"What were you doing in a dead girl's apartment?" asked Alan, still reeling from Erica's disclosure that she had visited Claudia's home.

"Just picking up a few things. At the request of the family."

"They asked for you?"

"No, Alan, they asked Dessie, and she asked me. And there was no yellow tape across the apartment door, so I guess it's no longer a crime scene."

"Erica, it never was a crime scene. She died at the People's Theater."

"But the body was moved," began Erica.

"Do you think someone killed her at her home, hailed a cab, and dropped her off in the lobby of the theater?"

"Probably not," said Erica. "Most cabbies balk at picking up mothers with strollers. A dead body would take a lot of explaining. Plus a significant tip. I'm just saying that if the apartment had been sealed, it was unsealed."

"You still didn't belong there," said Alan. "What if someone had walked in on you?"

"Who were you expecting?" asked Erica. "The police?"

"I'm sure they paid a visit at some point. It would be a place of interest to them."

"Thank you, Alan, for that skilled analysis," she said. "But I don't know that appearing on three episodes of *Law and Order* really qualifies you as an expert."

"But it was all three franchises," said Alan. "*Criminal Intent, Special Victims,* and the original," he added proudly. "Twice I played the defense attorney."

"Oh, well then. That qualifies you to practice law in several states."

"Only after I pass the bar," Alan said. "But, still, you had no business being there."

"Dessie asked me to," said Erica.

"And you can't say no to her?" asked Alan with rising concern in his voice.

"I don't think we're at that phase of our relationship," Erica responded.

"That's funny," said Alan. "We've always been at that phase in *our* relationship."

"Well, you're not in a supervisory capacity," Erica replied. Alan could only smile. "So you really think I was in some kind of jeopardy?" she continued.

"You would be, if the local authorities found you there," Alan answered.

"Well, no one did. I got in and out with no one seeing. The place was a disaster, by the way. Whoever went through it left things in a total mess."

"What do you think they were looking for?" Alan wanted to know.

"Beats me," said Erica. "If they found it, good luck to them. This place needed help on its best day. No light. Not a lot of air. And the décor was strictly from the sidewalk. Sad, sad, sad."

"Okay, it sounds like a depressing place," Alan agreed. "And I get the fact that your job is to ride shot gun on Dessie's excellent adventure. But remember—if Dessie's the one at the wheel, that puts you in the suicide seat."

"Do you think she's a danger to herself or to me?" asked Erica.

"No, of course not," Alan replied. "I think Dessie's a great gal. But did it ever occur to you not to listen to your master's voice when her requests become a little too bizarre to be believed?" he said.

"Maybe," said Erica. "This one did seem to cross a line. And maybe it was a yellow line. But it got me out of the office for most of the afternoon—"

"Is that what you're basing your decisions on these days?" he asked.

"No, Alan," said Erica firmly. "I'm not completely lacking in judgment. And I will be more careful in the future."

"Thank you," he answered. "That's all I ask."

There was a pause in the conversation before Alan said, "So, what did you find to send the family?"

"Well, there wasn't a lot to choose from," Erica answered. "A scarf. Some pieces of jewelry. Claudia was surprisingly skilled at beadwork, so there were a couple of pieces, finished and unfinished, that I sent the family," she continued. Not to mention a notebook that Erica would be keeping to herself for the time being.

"And how was your day?" she blithely inquired.

"Uneventful in comparison," said Alan.

"That's the theater for you," said Erica. "Never a dull moment."

CHAPTER 12

"It isn't beauty or personality or magnetism that makes a really
great actress. It is imagination, although these other qualities are
useful."
Laurette Taylor

About a month after the untimely demise of Claudia
Winthrop, Erica returned from one of her regular trips
to the library—this time to research the most frequently
used chamber pots in Renaissance Italy. Although the
pots themselves were considered quite beautiful, their
contents were tossed out of Renaissance windows to the
Renaissance streets below, leading to the less lovely
outcomes of plague and pestilence. Live and learn. As
Erica climbed the stairs to her office, she found herself
listening to the end of an unexpected but familiar
chorus.
"Happy Birthday to Ron,
Happy Birthday to you."
The birthday boy stood in the open area at the center
of his side of the building, surrounded by what
appeared to be every member of the army of the
ambitious. If the United States of Benneton were still a
nation, the work force of the People's Theater could
have been the center of their ad campaign, a coalition in
every shade of the rainbow. Bending over a flat,
rectangular cake, Ron uncoiled himself enough to blow
out the candles as he made a silent wish. As did the
choir who saluted him, although their wishes might
have run counter to his. What was particularly striking
was that each of the celebrants, from Ron on down, was

wearing his signature vinyl gloves. It was not immediately clear whether this was homage or ridicule.

Erica watched as Ron savored his unexpected moment in the sun, serving cake to the contingent forced to be his fans for an hour, giving a wink or a nod to those who had his special attention. She was reminded of Dessie's warning that Ron was eager to know everything about everybody. Thus far, his gaze had not landed on her, for which she was truly grateful. Her day might well come, but if and when it did, she was more than ready to fend him off, knowing full well that his desire to know her better was strictly informational. Her job at the People's Theater may have been Erica's first trip to this particular rodeo, but she was an experienced hand when it came to keeping her private life private, holding fast to the details, both personal and professional, that it was none of someone's—in this case, Ron's—business to know.

Yet, the upside to Ron was that he did know a lot about his co-workers, and he would make an excellent source of information should Erica decide she wanted to know more. Perhaps behind that unctuous exterior lay a person eager to share what he knew about the People's army, as well as their commanding officers, at a long and leisurely lunch. But at what cost? Erica was fairly certain that Ron would expect more in return than her picking up the check. Although she had not determined what he might be capable of, based on what she knew of him, she thought it would be in the ballpark of pretty much anything. This brought her reverie to an abrupt end as she shuddered at the idea of actually cozying up to Ron, regardless of what she might learn from him. That cake was not worth the candle.

Erica quickly returned to her office where she was greeted by Dessie.

"Oh, I'm sorry you missed the party," Dessie said.

"You folks are big into birthdays," Erica said.

"Not really," Dessie replied. "I just thought we could all use some cheering up. And this might be fun," she continued.

"It does have your fingerprints all over it. Or it would, if you weren't wearing gloves," said Erica. "And Ron? His would not be the birthday I'd think of as cause for celebration. Do you do this every year?"

"Well, no," said Dessie. "But his was the first one I came upon. And he does seem pleased."

"Strangely pleased," said Erica. "I can't believe I'm asking this again, but what's with the gloves?"

"Oh, we're just having a little fun with one of his quirks. For some reason, he seems to be enjoying the sight of a roomful of people with their hands covered in plastic."

"I think it's vinyl, Dessie," said Erica.

"Same difference," said Dessie. "And I'm enjoying it too." Dessie moved over to her desk. "Do you want a pair of gloves?" she asked. "We have plenty. I bought a couple of boxes—the giant economy size—I think there are about 25 pair in a box."

"No, thanks, I'll pass," said Erica.

"Would you like some cake?"

"Not really," said Erica. "I think I'll just get back to work."

"You should have seen our birthday celebrations in the old days," said Dessie, waxing nostalgic. "When *The Bros* was running full steam ahead, and we had plenty of money to work with. There would be champagne and lots of good eats. We would have paper masks made with the face of the birthday boy or girl on it. Everyone would wear one." Dessie stopped for a moment, then continued sadly. "Now it's plastic gloves and a supermarket cake."

"It's a step up from Claudia's cupcake," said Erica.

This reminder of the previous birthday celebration disrupted Dessie's reverie.

"Yes, well, Ron makes his presence felt around this place. I'm sure we'd miss him if he were gone," said Dessie.

"Shall we kill him and see?" asked Erica in an earnest tone.

Faintly unsettled by Erica's last comment, Dessie quickly recovered. "Well, fun's fun, but it's time to get back to work," she said.

"Yes, enough of this nonsense," Erica heartily agreed. "Onward," she said.

Later that same day, Erica and Dessie were making one of their regular trips to the copy room. They each held bundles of files, so Erica had insisted that they take the elevator, and Dessie had acquiesced. Unfortunately, the elevator was a slow mover on the best of days, and many people had the same idea. They were the last ones in, so they were closest to the door and the available air, but too many people in too little space made the short trip even longer. A loud phone conversation occurring by the back wall of the elevator interrupted the awkward silence.

"So, I told him, I said 'no way.' I'm not doing that. Not everything can be the way he wants it," insisted a female voice. She spoke at a level that made the phone redundant. They could probably hear her in Brooklyn. They could certainly hear her in this closed box. Needless to say, she was oblivious to anyone's discomfort but her own.

"So he said, fine. I'm done. It's my way or the highway," the speaker finished.

"That was original of him," said Dessie to Erica in a stage whisper no one missed.

"You know," Erica replied, "if someone said that to me, it would be my cue to head for the off-ramp."

When the elevator gently bounced to a stop, the speaker from the back pushed her way to the front, managing to bump into a record number of people on the way. One of them was Dessie. The speaker made no apologies, apparently having exhausted her vocal cords in the phone conversation. She might get away with being inconsiderate, but outright rudeness required more of a response. Dessie held the door as the young woman left the elevator.

"Excuse me," said Dessie. "Don't I know you?"

The speaker turned at the sound of a potential compliment, her aggrieved expression now radiantly transformed. "Maybe," she said. "I've done some Off-Broadway. I'm here to audition for *Michelangelo*."

"*Really*," said Dessie, sounding genuinely impressed. "Well, knock 'em dead. Oh, and what's your name?"

"Heather," the young woman proclaimed, in case anyone missed it. "Heather Maddox."

"Break a leg, Heather," said Dessie, as she took her hand off the elevator door, allowing it to close. The remaining members of the assembled multitude breathed a sigh of relief as the elevator began to move again.

"Heather Maddox," said Dessie to Erica, when they finally reached the desired floor and were disgorged from the elevator. "I'm going to the casting office when we finish in the copy room. Heather is toast."

"Whew, that's a pretty severe punishment for rudeness," said Erica. "Why would you do that?"

"Because I can," answered Dessie.

"Remind me never to cross you," said Erica.

"You don't need to be reminded. That's why we work so well together," said Dessie, as she pushed on to her destination.

CHAPTER 13

"Always be smarter than the people who hire you."
Lena Horne

After a decent interval had elapsed, Dessie decided it was time to find a replacement for Claudia. Interestingly, as much as Claudia's desk enjoyed a prime location, no one much wanted Claudia's job, including Zack, who had done no politicking to get closer to the seat of power, evidently finding no reason to revisit the scene of his curious flirtation. Briefly of interest to the authorities once his "Are you still here?" had been reported, Zack was alibied by Zeke and Christy, with whom he had been fomenting revolution in a coffee shop—and they had the selfies to prove it. It was quickly concluded that this may have been a case of misguided ambition but hardly a motive for murder, and Zack was dismissed as a suspect. There had been no politicking, a least none that Erica had witnessed. This seemed to be less about respect for the dead than the lack of desire on anyone's part to be the new Claudia. But someone needed to take the curse off the seat.

Dessie may have done a careful search or simply pulled a name out of a hat; either way, her choice was a surprise. A slight Latina, given to fits of enthusiasm whenever Lin-Manuel Miranda's name was mentioned, became the chosen one. Her name was Montserrat.

If Asha and Chloe wore understated designer originals, Monteserrat wore the knock offs of knock offs. Monty, as she preferred to be known—she was also a fan of old movies and had a thing for Montgomery Clift—took a long subway ride from the Bronx each morning to the very downtown People's Theater. After work, instead of hanging out in faux dive bars on the Lower East Side, Monty headed home to cook dinner for three younger siblings, two sisters and a brother, before her mother headed out to clean an office building, and her father got home from his day job, laying track for the Second Avenue subway, and went off to his night job, on guard duty at a bodega. Living at home allowed Monty to get by on the small salary she received from the People's Theater. She had her parents' blessing, as neither had the heart to place a limit on their daughter's dreams, which was just as well. No one could.

Perhaps Dessie saw some of her own determination in Monty, and this led to Monty's promotion. In any case, without consulting Alex, which she rarely did anyway, Dessie put Monty into Claudia's chair. Given that Monty was a quick study, technologically savvy, and had no desire to scribble in marble notebooks, she would seem to be a slam dunk. She and Dessie worked together happily for the better part of a week, a week in which Alex was attending a theater conference at Princeton.

On the morning of her return, as Alex swept through the office, Monty looked up and gave her boss a bright and clear-eyed "good morning." Alex took one look at Monty and promptly fired her. Monty was not simply sent back to her previous job at the People's Theater, keeping track of group sales figures. She was out.

"Was it something she said?" asked Erica, as she and Dessie commiserated a few hours later in a far-off corner of the theater.

"She didn't have time to say anything beyond 'good morning,'" Dessie replied. "Poor Monty was devastated. I was stunned. I just spent most of my morning calling theaters to find her something else."

"Did Alex have something against her? Did she even know her?" asked Erica.

"Not to my knowledge on both counts," Dessie answered. "The official excuse was that Alex had not been consulted about this change, although she never questioned any of my hiring decisions before."

"That's comforting," said Erica. "But why is Alex taking this out on poor Monty?"

"Well, before we cry too many tears for poor Monty," Dessie said, "let me just say that Monty has always wanted to go into casting. After the tale of her unceremonious dumping was shared, she was offered a job as a casting assistant at a slightly higher salary and a whole lot more prestige. All those would-be actors in the People's army will soon be knocking on Monty's door. An added advantage to having Monty on board is the opportunity to hear firsthand how Alexa Wallace fired an underling without cause or provocation. That would be too delicious to pass up."

"Did Alex even apologize?"

"I don't think so," said Dessie dismissively. "An apology to someone may have been in order, but Monty was quickly whisked from the premises."

"Well, it sounds like Monty made out okay," said Erica. "I was thinking more in terms of you."

Dessie looked genuinely surprised. "When Alex apologizes to me for anything, Erica, I'll call you," she said. "After I alert the media. I promise."

"Good to know," said Erica. "But still, I wonder what's going on. Alex is usually so under control. If anything, too controlled. Has she ever done anything like this?"

"No," said Dessie.

"And?" asked Erica.

"And, nothing to add," said Dessie. "She's always been the same cool customer. And she certainly had nothing against Monty," Dessie added. "Alex was the one who insisted that I start calling theaters to get her something else."

"Then why?" Erica insisted. "Was she planning to turn that desk into a shrine?"

"I hope not," said Dessie. "We don't have the space to waste. All she said was that I should have checked with her first."

"That *would* be a first," said Erica. "So what are you going to do?" she asked.

"Keep the desk empty," said Dessie. "Hire no one for a very long time, and check with Alex first. At least on this one. Oh, and Erica?"

"Yes?" said Erica, sensing what was coming.

"I'm going to need you to help me out," Dessie said.

"You're making me the new Claudia?" Erica asked.

"No, there'll be none of that," said Dessie. "You're still Erica, still in your regular spot. But I'm going to need you to cover some of Claudia's responsibilities."

"Claudia had responsibilities?"

"Well, I don't know, her tasks, little jobs, chores. You're the professor, you pick the words."

"Keeping on that theme, I'm comfortable with 'assignments,'" said Erica. Maybe 'commissions.' 'Missions,' if things get complicated."

"Fine," said Dessie. "Missions, it is. Just understand this. You're mine."

"Yes, ma'am," said Erica briskly, thinking Dessie was kidding, but seeing from her expression that she was not. "I think I understand," Erica said, more carefully.

"As long as you do," Dessie calmly replied.

CHAPTER 14

"What the mother sings to the cradle goes all the way to the coffin."
Henry Ward Beecher

After the excitement of the morning, Erica took a late lunch, retreating with her turkey sandwich to a bench in a nearby park. The weather was barely warm enough for a picnic, but what she needed more than fresh air was a little time and space away from the inquiring eyes of her co-workers. Not that most of them paid any attention to her beyond a polite exchange of pleasantries. She knew that she had been deemed agreeable but of no particular usefulness to anyone's career, not meriting any significant investment of time. Erica felt much the same way about most of them. So she sat alone and read Claudia's notebook in the fading sunlight.

The blunt repetition in Volume One had given way to a series of journal entries in Volume Two that carefully accounted for Claudia's activities over the last few years. Rather than taking a you-are-there approach, Claudia opted for just the facts, which had all the excitement of a laundry list. Erica began to speed read through the content, which still managed to hold her interest.

To begin with, Claudia's parents had never told her that she was adopted, and she was none too pleased about that. This is never a good idea—think what it did to Oedipus—but Claudia's parents were probably not thinking about the tragic end of the King of Thebes when they decided to skip that useful bit of information. Apparently, the distance between farm houses and the natural reticence of New Englanders kept their secret safe. At least until a stretch of black ice on a lonely country road put an abrupt end to the people who had raised Claudia. Over eighteen at the time of the accident, Claudia had been at home and out of harm's way. The sympathetic aunt and uncle descended upon her shortly after the funeral, but as a legal adult, she shooed them away to begin a solitary journey through her parents' belongings. Although she wasn't looking for anything in particular, in the attic, she stumbled upon the mother lode. Only two feet from where she had played dress up was a dented trunk with a broken lock. With her natural lack of curiosity, she had previously ignored it. Looking inside, she found the incontrovertible evidence that these people were not her biological parents—an idea she had not given serious consideration to since she was eight and going through a fairy-princess phase.

Making her way through a stack of yellowing papers, Claudia had discovered that her parents, these two kindly people to whom she bore no physical resemblance, had, indeed, adopted her. It was a private adoption, without the aid or intrusion of an agency. A country lawyer with a local address—long gone, as Claudia would soon discover—had handled the paperwork. The trunk held both the petition to adopt and the final decree of adoption. Claudia had seen her birth certificate, which listed the Winthrops as her parents, but this was an amended version, in keeping with the laws of most states at the time, as she would later learn. The infant Claudia had come into their lives two days after the date of her birth and remained there until their premature death. Claudia might never had known the truth, unless she needed a kidney and neither one was a compatible donor. That would have been an interesting conversation. But then and there, Claudia decided, it was up to her to find the truth about her biological parents—who they were and why they had given her up.

This question was quickly answered with a little more digging into the trunk. Claudia's birth mother had left a thank-you note of sorts. It read,

> I want to thank you for taking the baby. I know you will be good to her. Giving birth to her was the hardest thing I've ever done. I am going back to my life before. I have worked too hard to give it up now. It will be best for me and best for her. Thank you for the money. It will get me back to where I want to be, to the only life I have ever wanted.

From the yellowed square of tape on the page, Erica could see where the note had once been pasted, but the space was now empty. Ever diligent, Claudia had neatly transcribed it into her journal. The message was brisk and to the point, honest and unsentimental, and most importantly, unsigned. Although there are cards for every occasion, Hallmark would not be calling any time soon to adopt the sentiment.

There was no sign of regret in giving up the daughter she had just given birth to. Not "my baby," but "the baby." "It will be best for me" came before what was "best for her." And all those "I's." There was no mention of Claudia's father, his involvement, or his interest in the child. Did he give up his parental rights? Did he even know he was a parent? The birth mother had wanted to go on with her life without the child that would keep her from living it. And the Winthrops had helped to pay her way there. Was it generosity on their part, or something closer to a bribe? Clearly, they were keepers of papers—they had not discarded the note, even with its distinct lack of family feeling—but Claudia had found no cancelled check. Did they pay for their child in cash? And kept no receipt? Upon reading the note, Claudia immediately narrowed her search: she would find the mother who had relinquished her, and done so without a backward glance.

"I will find her," Claudia wrote, in her flailing scrawl. "I will never give up. I will keep her note forever. It will remind me of what she did. I will hate her forever."

Well, thought Erica, *like her mother, Claudia gets right to the point. Who knew that writing styles could be inherited?* She read on.

According to her journal, Claudia chose to discuss this with no one; after all, no one had discussed it with her. Erica wondered why Claudia did not turn to the aunt and uncle, the only people in the world who seemed to care about her, but Claudia's distrust seeped into her writing. She blamed them for not telling her the truth and doubted they would have any help to give, choosing instead to pursue the search on her own, keeping it secret. Being a child of the computer age, she knew where to start. Claudia might prefer marble notebooks for her private writing, but she could work a public space as well as any of her peers.

Erica had to admit that Claudia was thorough and wrote everything down. As a result, her journal provided quite an education in adoptions. Erica learned that in the 1930's, for example, when a child was adopted, a new birth certificate was issued, listing the adoptive parents as the natural parents. Before World War II, both the original birth certificate and the amended version were available to the adopted child and to either set of parents. With the postwar baby boom, these documents were sealed in most states, both to the parent in search of a child, and to the child in search of a parent. When Claudia began her search, only a few states—Alabama, Alaska, Kansas, and Oregon—allowed adoptees to see their birth certificate when they reached legal age. New Hampshire quickly followed. Unfortunately for Claudia, she lived in none of these states.

So she took to the internet, using sites like the provocatively named *Bastard Nation*, which kept her updated on pending legislation regarding disclosure laws in the remaining forty-five states. The National Adoption Clearinghouse gave her a state-by-state listing of which agencies could provide her with the information to aid her search. And then there were the private searchers. For a substantial fee, Claudia could hire a Confidential Intermediary, or CI, someone sanctioned by a court to open the sealed adoption files. The arrangement brokered by the CI could be anything from an exchange of medical histories to an exchange of addresses if the object of the search was willing to divulge his or her name or whereabouts. From there, the goal would be to arrange a reunion. The CI's fees were collected in advance and were non-refundable. If the search could not be completed due to the death or disinterest of the party in question, the person paying for the search was out of luck. When Claudia learned that the CI was in no way accountable for the success of the search, she decided to pass. There was also the risk that the CI's advances would be rejected, when the first contact, coming from the child, might not be refused. There were even "adoption angels" out there, willing to assist searchers for the heavenly cost of nothing.

Being more of a do-it-yourself-er, Claudia was not willing to sit and wait. Still, she could see that however she approached the search, it would cost money, possibly a lot of it. Ignoring the emotional toll it might take on her, Claudia focused on the finances. She sold the homestead that had been left to her—lock, stock and livestock—to a couple of yuppies who thought it might be fun to run a farm. They didn't make it to the first harvest, but Claudia had her seed money, enabling her to rent a small room in the center of town. She held on to her job as a checker at the local supermarket so no one would think that anything about Claudia, beyond her address, had changed.

Erica put down the notebook for a moment to get her bearings. She could not square the searcher with the search. The vitriol of Volume One had given way to the relative calm of Volume Two. Claudia's words revealed no emotional investment in the search, as if this experience, with its potential to change her life, was happening to someone else. Who was Claudia? What was she? Was she fastidious or a flake? Or simply a fake? Neither the choler of Volume One nor the calm of Volume Two sounded like the Claudia that Erica had seen at work. Could there have been another actor in their midst—a good one at that—running loose in the halls of the People's Theater? Lacking an answer to that question, Erica returned to her reading.

Like many adoptees, a major event in her life—the death of the Winthrops—had served as the catalyst for Claudia's decision to search for her birth mother. The emotional implications were a little different, given that she'd only recently learned that she had been adopted. Similar to many adoptees, Claudia, in her way, felt she was taking charge of her life, seizing control of a situation that had been determined for her when she was born. In Claudia's case, this was amplified by the Winthrops' decision to shelter her from both the fact and knowledge of her adoption. But they were gone, and she could not turn to them—in her journals, she seemed to have turned on them—so she was way past the point of any residual family feeling. Claudia revealed no particular concern about her genetic history: she was perfectly healthy and still at an age when she thought herself invincible. She had no particular interest in adding herself to a family tree. All she wanted was a name, not so much to see a face, but simply to know a name. And with that name should come a reason, an explanation beyond a brief note, as to why this woman had abandoned her child.

Erica doubted that a combination of words existed to convince Claudia of the rightness of her mother's path, or that Claudia was better off the way things had turned out. She also wondered why neither Claudia's search nor her anger was directed toward the birth father. For some reason, he was off her radar and consequently off the hook.

Checking her watch, Erica could see that the hour was ending, so she read faster. Claudia had begun as what is known as a passive searcher, but, from her extensive adoption reading list, Claudia learned that she needed to make herself "findable." There were sites that tried to connect parents and children—at last count, they numbered in the hundreds—and Claudia found her way to more than a few of them. For several months, Claudia dutifully typed in her essential information— name, birth date, place of birth—hoping that her birth mother cruised these same sites and would initiate contact. She signed up at mutual-consent registries, which ask for the sex of the child, the birth date, place of birth, and the name of the place where the adoption took place, in hopes that someone would contact her. For the better part of a year, she sent out the call, but no one answered.

Claudia decided that a more direct approach was needed.

She needn't have bothered.

CHAPTER 15

"If people knew how hard I worked to get my mastery, it wouldn't
seem so wonderful at all."
Michelangelo

That evening, as Erica left work for the day, she
came upon an unusual sight. She had taken to leaving
the theater by way of the back exit, following the route
that Dessie had shown her on the day after Claudia's
murder, when they were trying to avoid the paparazzi
assembled on the sidewalk in front of the theater. As
Erica turned into the alley that led to the street, she was
almost hit by flying garbage coming from the dumpster
that sat a few feet from the theater exit. Spewing forth
was a variety of projectiles, from the corner of a
wooden picture frame, to the metal wheel from the
bottom of a cart, to a piece of drop cloth spattered with
blue and green paint. But no projectors did Erica see—
no one doing the actual tossing.

When there was a break in the action, Erica moved
closer to the dumpster to peer over the side, letting
whoever was inside know she was there.

"Hey, can you stop a minute?" said Erica. "There are
people walking out here."

From the belly of the beast emerged a face partially
obscured by a beard, followed by shoulders encased in
flannel.

"Hey, sorry," he said, sounding genuinely
apologetic. "Did we hit you?"

"Missed me by that much," said Erica, showing him
a small space between her thumb and index finger.

"You don't look like a dumpster diver. What are you looking for?"

"What does a dumpster diver look like?" asked a second voice. A second body emerged from the container, this one smaller, female, and markedly less hairy that her co-worker.

"Starving," said Erica. "And desperate."

"Oh, we're desperate," said the male half of the duo. "Or at least, one of us is," he added, giving his associate a look that left no doubt as to who got them into this predicament.

"Sorry, sorry, sorry," she said. "How many times can I say it? So kill me." She turned to Erica to explain. "We're on the props crew for *Michelangelo*. I threw out—*by mistake*," she said, directing this to her partner in crime—"a genuine copy of an original Michelangelo—a painting in miniature—that they use in the show."

"Oh," said Erica, suddenly interested. "Was it a copy of the first picture that Michelangelo ever painted?" she asked. "I read about it in the *Times*."

The hunters looked blank.

"It's a *newspaper*," Erica explained.

They looked blanker still.

"You hold it in your hands and read it at the same time," Erica insisted.

"I know what the *Times* is," the male hunter replied. "I read it online. For the reviews."

His accomplice nodded in agreement.

"Okay, then," said Erica. "Well, in case you missed the article, this painting is supposed to be Michelangelo's first painting, done when he was about 12 or 13. He copied a print of a German engraving called *St. Anthony Tormented by Demons*. There was a mangy bunch of demons swirling around poor St. Anthony—they had wings, tails, scales—"

"Scales?" interjected the female hunter.

"Yes, in fact," Erica confirmed. "Apparently, Michelangelo bought fish at the local fish market to get the scales just right."

"And what did he copy to get the demons just right?" her male companion wanted to know.

"His bad dreams, probably," said Erica.

"But he copied?" asked the female half of the team, in a plaintive plea.

"Well, yes," said Erica, "but I think we're in the area known as the sincerest form of flattery. In those days, an artist just starting out would copy more accomplished painters, and it wouldn't be considered stealing. When they got really good, artists would compete with each other, painting the same scene and showing how it should be done, according to the artist's distinctive style. But that's a ways away for young Michelangelo at this point in his career."

The two hunters had stopped their work, standing at rapt attention as they listened to Erica. The once and former teacher was pleased.

Still got it, she thought.

"So, is it a copy of the first Michelangelo that you lost?" Erica asked.

The two shrugged in unison.

"I don't know," said the man in charge.

"I don't remember," said his assistant. "It was small and painted and I didn't really look at the picture," she said.

"It's essential to the scene, though," said the first hunter, whose voice was somewhat obscured by his return to rooting around in the dumpster. "They paid somebody a lot of money to make that copy. For the *authenticity*," he added, enjoying the word.

"Oh, yeah, like the audience can really tell if it's an authentic copy or if I scribbled a stick figure on a piece of cardboard. It won't *read*," his female counterpart said, with her own emphasis.

"*Read* means the audience won't be able to see it," the male searcher explained, directing this to Erica.

"I know what *read* means," said Erica.

Ignoring her response, he continued, this time speaking in the direction of his associate. "And it doesn't really matter if the audience can see it. The actors can tell the difference, and that's what matters. It helps with their performance," he said, again speaking to Erica.

"Unhuh," Erica replied, seeing that her ignorance was a given as far as he was concerned.

"And if we don't find it, the stage manager will have our heads," he finished.

"Mine, you mean," said his companion.

"Both of ours," he insisted. "You are under my supervision."

"Jurisdiction is more like it," she muttered, once again submerging herself in the trash.

"Don't tell me you're rooting around down there without any protective clothing?" Erica asked, peeking over the side of the dumpster.

"No way," said the two, popping up in unison as they almost bumped heads. They presented their hands in a pose that would make Bob Fosse proud. Two pair of jazz hands were close enough to Erica's face for her to see that they were covered by the vinyl gloves that had become so familiar to her.

"There are loads of these all over the theater," the female half of the team said. "You can find boxes of them everywhere."

"So I'm beginning to see," said Erica. "Well, gotta go," she quickly added. "Keep up the good work. And good luck," she called to them, as she made her way down the street, stepping over the rubble strewn along the alley.

"Duck!" was the reply, shouted by the female voice, as a square black projectile nearly hit the left side of Erica's head, brushing her hair as it flew by.

"That's not a frisbee, dude!" she yelled to her male co-worker, who had now begun flinging objects out of the dumpster, seemingly with no thought of who might still be in the vicinity.

"Sorry, lady," he said, sounding truly penitent. "I thought you were gone."

"Not quite," said Erica, moving a little more quickly in the direction of the street. She turned away from them and looked down at the object that had nearly sideswiped her. It was a square black cardboard notebook, the kind some people use to scribble their hopes, their dreams. Their death threats.

"Oh, no," Erica moaned, bending down to retrieve it. She opened the marble notebook, and sure enough, it was Claudia's. Volume One. The one Erica had given to Dessie for safekeeping, with the promise that Dessie would hand it over to the police. *Would they have returned this piece of evidence, finding it irrelevant to the investigation?* Erica wondered. *The case was far from closed, but with no suspects and waning interest, would the authorities have rejected a possible lead? In any case, what was it doing in the dumpster?*

As she quickly flipped through the pages, Erica could see that it was none the worse for wear. She brushed off the cover to remove any traces of refuse; if they existed, they were invisible to the naked eye. Without a good bye, she left the searchers to their work.

CHAPTER 16

> "No poem or play or song
> Can fully right a wrong
> Inflicted and endured."
> Seamus Heaney, *The Cure at Troy*

"You did what?" asked Alan, when Erica finally made it home that evening.

"Alan, you're repeating yourself," Erica said.

"So are you," Alan replied. "Erica, what were you thinking? You're telling me that you took Claudia's notebook out of her apartment? And kept it? I'm pretty sure that's a little thing called withholding evidence."

For the time being, Erica chose to withhold the fact that she had more than one of Claudia's notebooks in her possession. Instead, she said, "Ah, that *Law and Order* training comes through again. And, okay, yes, it could be seen that way."

"It's not up to you to pick and choose what's evidence and what's not," Alan continued, with some exasperation.

"It was up to me to decide what to send the family," said Erica calmly, hoping to defuse the situation. "Do you really think they wanted to read a notebook spewing venom from their dear departed niece? It could be seen as an act of kindness on my part," she rationalized.

"That's mighty self-serving of you," Alan said. "Not to mention," he continued, "that you were going to stay away from this one. You remember, laying low?"

"I do," said Erica. "And, believe me, the more I learn about Claudia, the harder she is to warm up to."

"Then why are you involved in this?"

"Does it really matter, Alan?"

"Quite a lot, as a matter of fact," he answered.

"Because she was twenty-something," said Erica. "And she didn't get to be twenty-something more."

"Oh, well then. That's reason enough, then, to risk, I don't know, your job," said Alan, with increasing irritation.

Erica said nothing.

"I thought we already had this little talk," he said. "Just because Dessie says it, doesn't make it so. She and the justice system may have a slightly different sense of what's appropriate behavior. Possibly even legal."

"I am of the same opinion," Erica said. "But for the time being, could we look at this as an act of charity? And can I please tell you what I've found?" she implored.

"Do I have a choice?" Alan asked.

"There's always a choice," said Erica. "So listen up."

"That's my choice?" he said. But Erica had already begun.

"Once upon a time, there was a girl named Claudia."

"Give me the anecdote," he insisted. "Not the saga."

Erica complied. She hit the highlights of Claudia's tale, from her days down on the farm to the trunk that belched its secrets to the search for the mother that Claudia reviled. Erica saved the best for last.

"According to her journal, Claudia had all the preliminary research done, as much as she could do while sitting in her little room."

"Not exactly aggressive, was she?" said Alan.

"Well, it took her some time, but she got there. You wouldn't have known it to look at her, but she was one angry girl. And she funneled that anger into her search. She went to all the usual sites. *Bastard Nation*, for one."

"It's called what?" Alan sputtered.

"You heard me. And she was just about ready to invest everything she had into the search. I'm talking emotional as well as financial. Then she didn't have to."

"Why not?" he inquired. "Did her mom magically appear on her doorstep?"

"No, but maybe the next best thing. Dessie told me that Claudia came from a small town. In Maine, actually. And the funny thing is—well, I'm not so sure Claudia was laughing—but Maine recently changed the laws regarding adult adoptees. I checked, and it's true. Now, if you were adopted in the state of Maine, all you need is a completed application, a notarized birth certificate, the fee and—ta dah—the good people in Augusta will send you your original birth certificate. The one with your birth name on it. Or more to the point, the one with your birth parents' names on it, not the names of your adoptive parents, as is the case in most of the fifty states."

"And Claudia sent for hers?"

"She must have," said Erica. "From the privacy of her own home, she found out who her parents were. No muss, no fuss. Well, obviously some fuss. With the lottery, they say that all it takes is a dollar and a dream. This costs twenty-five dollars plus an extra-long envelope and postage. And it's guaranteed to change your life."

"Don't keep me in suspense," Alan inquired. "Anyone we know?"

"You won't believe it," said Erica.

"Try me," he said.

"Well, Claudia was pretty pissed off that her birth mother didn't even name her. She goes on for a few pages about how she was listed as 'Baby Girl' on her original birth certificate."

"Okay, but that's not the name we're looking for. What was her birth mother's name?"

"I don't know," said Erica. "She ran out of space."

"Come on," Alan began.

"No, really," Erica countered. "At the bottom of the last page, it says—"

"It says, 'Dear Diary, My mother is—oh, never mind?'"

"No, Alan, not exactly," Erica replied. "After carefully detailing the whole process, Claudia finishes with, 'Now I know. And I know where to find her. And I will.'"

"The end?" he asked.

"The end," Erica finished. "Once she knew, that was all that mattered. Why buy a new notebook for a two-word name? There was more than a little of the thrifty Yankee in Claudia."

"And you have no idea who she was looking for?" Alan asked.

"Not yet," Erica admitted. "But she did land on the doorstep of the People's Theater. And without a trace of a New England accent, come to think of it," Erica added. "As little as she said. Not a trace of an accent on anyone's part," she repeated, mostly to herself.

"So what do you plan to do?" Alan asked.

"Return to Plan A," Erica answered. "Resume the position. The one we previously discussed. The one where I lay low."

"Excellent choice, my dear," said Alan. "When do you begin?"

"How about now?" said Erica. "Will you join me?"

CHAPTER 17

"Ideal stage managers not only need to be calm and meticulous
professionals who know their craft, but masochists who feel pride
in rising above impossible odds."
Peter Hall

The next morning, an unknown figure stood outside
Alex's office, leaning on the desk that had been vacated
by Claudia, and shortly thereafter by Monty. It stood
about six feet tall, wearing a flannel shirt with no
obvious connection to the grunge movement, jeans and
work boots, along with a watch with a fat brown leather
strap, the signifier of the technical staff. And it was a
woman.

"Get Alex out here!" she bellowed.

Given how little bellowing rang through the halls of
the People's Theater—it was strictly forbidden, at least
outside the rehearsal rooms—the sound brought Erica
out of her own office and into Dessie's. Dessie was
nowhere in sight.

"Can I do anything for you?" asked Erica, regretting
the words as soon as they came out of her mouth.

"Oh, baby, I hope so," was the woman's reply. "As I
said," she repeated in a somewhat modulated tone, "get
Alex out here."

At that moment, Dessie appeared in the doorway of
Alex's office and seemed ready to hurl all five feet of
her poundage directly at the woman causing the
disturbance. It would have been an interesting match
up, but the bout was abruptly scratched. Instead, Alex
got herself out there.

"Get in here, Suzie Q," said Alex. Suzie Q quickly obliged.

"Suzie Q?" Erica whispered to Dessie when the coast was clear. "As in 'Baby, I love you'?"

Dessie shook her head to indicate the negative. "She's the stage manager for *Michelangelo*," Dessie said. "I don't get it, but Alex uses her on all our big productions. She did *The Brothers Wittgenstein*, from workshop to Broadway." Dessie looked in the direction of Alex's door. "She must be good at what she does," Dessie continued, "or Alex wouldn't keep using her." She shook her head again. "Her appeal is lost on me."

It was a short meeting. Alex and Suzie quickly emerged, with Suzie's voice being heard to say, "And I'm going to kill those numbskulls who tossed that picture in the trash."

"They found it, didn't they?" said Alex coolly.

"Yes," replied Suzie in her usual brusque tone.

"Well, a little forgiveness goes a long way," Alex offered.

"Not far enough."

"Suzie," Alex replied pointedly, "let it be."

"Okay, fine," Suzie snapped. "Next topic. I don't care if you call them actors or actresses, they still pee sitting down."

"Suzie, let's remember we're using our indoor voices," said Alex. "And many females prefer to be referred to as actors, the gender-neutral term—"

"Oh, spare me the political correctness," Suzie answered.

"Even so, we have to respect their choices," said Alex. "So call them what they want to be called," she added, more firmly this time.

"Fine, fine, they're all actors," said Suzie, dismissing her defeat. "But what are you going to do about the *actor*, and by this I mean the guy, playing

Michelangelo's good-for-nothing father? He's got the good-for-nothing down, I'll give him that."

This was far too much information for even a semi-public forum, and Alex moved to squash the discussion.

"Until such time as I hear from the *director* that changes need to be made, changes will not be made. Changes will not even be suggested by anyone other than the director. Do I make myself clear?"

"As always, Alex," Suzie smiled, enjoying their little joust, even if she seemed to come out on the losing end. "It's a pleasure doing business with you," she said, as she prepared to leave the office.

"Dessie," Suzie said, nodding in her direction. Dessie had resumed her seat and busied herself, barely acknowledging the greeting.

Suzie turned to Erica. "And you, whoever you are. I hope we meet again."

Suzie laughed and left before Erica had a chance to speak.

"My best to Vin and the kids," said Alex, as the figure of Suzie receded in the distance. Alex then returned to her office without a word to anyone else.

"Vin and the kids?" whispered Erica to Dessie.

"Never judge a book by its cover," said Dessie, who rejoined the conversation only after Suzie's departure.

"Or its come-ons," said Erica.

CHAPTER 18

"For an actress to be a success, she must have the face of Venus,
the brains of Minerva, the grace of Terpischore, the memory of
Macaulay, the figure of Juno, and the hide of a rhinoceros."
Ethel Barrymore

Michelangelo already had a mom, he even had a younger version of himself. In fact, the actors playing these roles were deep into rehearsal before the man himself—the lead role—was cast. As Dessie had promised, there was a first-act duet, and it was stunning. Musically it was everything the composer had dreamed, and there would not be a dry eye in the house as mother and young son went at it, pouring out their mutual longing before they faced a long separation, a separation that would last for the rest of their lives. The reality was even harsher. In life, young Michelangelo barely knew his mother and harbored mostly ill will toward her, making this tearful good bye an event entirely the creation of the playwright. In another case of life approximating art, the mother and son in rehearsal quickly came to loathe each other.

Young Bobby Beasley had been a theater veteran from the age of three when he was carried onstage as the changeling boy at the end of a production of *A Midsummer Night's Dream*—the definitive changeling boy, according to one reviewer. Since his humble beginning as a plot device and human prop, Bobby had eight years to hone his craft, and at age eleven he knew every trick in the book. The farewell scene was blocked to place him in a downstage position, so his mother's face would be the one seen by the audience. In rehearsal, Bobby began to edge ever so slightly upstage, trying to force his scene and singing partner, dear old mom, the more famous Miranda Owen, out of position. Miranda could either sing to thin air as her son disappeared from her range of vision, or turn to the skulking boy, thus turning her face away from the audience and her back to it. In television, actors had to stay where they were told, to accommodate the camera angles. In theater, actors had more room to roam. While young Bobby could be corrected by the director or threatened by the stage manager during rehearsals, who knew what he might try during a performance?

Miranda might not have been on the stage in a while, but this was not her first trip to the rodeo. Their duet was turning into a duel: so far, it was a draw. Still, this was more of a workout than she expected. Initially, Miranda had complained when her character disappeared before intermission. Now, she began to look forward to sitting out the second act and waiting for the curtain call, although she would not be going quietly to her dressing room to make dinner reservations. Instead, she came up with a creative solution to the Bobby problem.

She did nothing.

As Bobby, in all his boyish glee, attempted to make Miranda turn away from the audience, she ignored him. He could dance and skip and make adorable faces, but she saw none of it, choosing instead to leave him to his own devices, as he floated upstage. To all eyes, she appeared to handle it graciously, shrugging ever so slightly, in a gesture that telegraphed to the audience that "boys will be boys." Her move killed at rehearsal and everyone agreed that she should keep it in.

Offstage, Miranda could afford to be more direct. One of America's favorite TV moms, currently enjoying a spot just below Mrs. Cunningham and above Donna Reed on *E! Entertainment*'s list of the top 100, demanded that her onstage son—the brat, as she charitably referred to him—be out of her sight and her sightlines unless they were onstage. Her celebrity trumped Bobby's tearful pleas that he was innocent of the charge—tears he had been trained to deliver. While the management could not officially agree to such a demand, when it came time to assign dressing rooms, Bobby, even with a featured role, found himself sequestered in the farthest reaches of the theater, sharing a make-up mirror with the gentlemen of the ensemble, who tripled up on speaking parts and counter space. Bobby was not happy, but it was a lesson that would stand him in good stead: never take on someone more famous than you, or you could find yourself in dressing-room Siberia.

CHAPTER 19

"The actor does not need to 'become' the character. The phrase, in fact, has no meaning. There *is* no character. There are only lines upon a page. They are lines of dialogue meant to be said by the actor. When he or she says them simply, in an attempt to achieve an object more or less like that suggested by the author, the audience sees an *illusion* of the character."
David Mamet

"The good news is, we have our Michelangelo," said Dessie.

"Hooray!" Erica said. "That's a great way to start the day. Who is he?"

"It's Kenneth Garrison," Dessie announced.

"Kenny! I love him," said Erica, with almost a squeal in her voice.

"Does Alan know?" asked Dessie impishly.

"He should," said Erica. "He introduced me to Kenny. In fact, he dragged me out to New Jersey a couple of months ago to see his old buddy in a production of *1776*. Which I also love, by the way. I just can't get enough of our forefathers strutting their stuff. The signing of the Declaration of Independence in song and dance. Gotta love it."

Erica waited for Dessie to tell her which one of the two—count them, two—female roles (in a cast of twenty six) that she had played in the musical about the founding of America. Similar to the women living in 1776, she had played none.

"I love it too, as a matter of fact," said Dessie. "Which one was Kenny?"

"Well, let's think. He has that intensity that some slightly shorter men have."

"Slightly shorter than what? Not me," said Dessie.

"Shorter than the national average," said Erica. "Not short—"

"Like me," said Dessie.

"Good things, small packages, let's leave it at that," Erica insisted.

"If I had a nickel for every time—"

It was Erica's turn to cut her off. "You haven't guessed yet, Dessie," she said.

"Oh, he was John Adams, of course," Dessie replied.

"You are good at this," Erica said.

"I know," said Dessie.

"I do like that show," Erica repeated. "And I can only imagine what it was like to hear the Declaration of Independence read for the first time. It must have been unbelievably powerful. I wish I could have seen it."

"I always wish I could have seen Angela Lansbury in *Mame*," said Asha, as always with Chloe. The pair had entered Dessie's office to deposit a single folder on her desk. "Now that must have been great," Asha finished.

"I wish I could know the future," said Chloe.

"No, you don't," said Erica and Dessie together. Asha and Chloe politely smiled the same smile, the one that said they knew better than these well-meaning but mistaken ladies, and left the room in their own form of unison.

"The 1970's," Dessie said to Erica after they had gone. "Like the 1770's. Ancient history."

"To each his own historic moment," said Erica. "Anyway, I'm glad they cast Kenny. I've met a lot of actors through Alan, and some of them seem more comfortable when they're playing a part—more at ease in someone else's skin. Alan isn't like that—he can work it either way—and I'd say the same for Kenny. He's what Alan calls an actor's actor."

"Martin was like that," said Dessie wistfully. "Comfortable as himself and as a character."

"I bet he was," said Erica, once again choosing to be tactful.

"And sometimes, you have to do more than look the part," said Dessie. "You have to play the part."

"What did Michelangelo look like?" asked Erica.

"Like Kenny, I guess," answered Dessie, completely serious. "And he is exactly the kind of casting that the People's Theater is all about. I admit we do our share of stunt casting—movie stars on holiday, although they usually find that they've never worked so hard in their lives. But this guy is the real deal. He may not be well known outside the theater, but he's extremely well respected in it. His work is detailed, right down to his shoe laces. I know he'll be great," Dessie finished.

"Yes," said Erica. "He doesn't seem to be one of those actors who prepares for a role by living the part. You know the type. If he's going to play a Native American from way back when, he learns to hunt, fish, and skin animals with a sharp rock tied to a stick."

"That always comes in handy," said Dessie.

"Or if the character has just been beaten up—"

"Don't finish that thought," said Dessie. "It reminds me of someone, I won't say who. She came in to read for *Michelangelo*. The last thing I saw her in, she played a character who was filing assault charges. Those bruises looked way too real."

"Kudos to the make-up man?" asked Erica.

"I'd like to think so," said Dessie. "But she's well known for her commitment to a role. If she were cast as a nun, she'd join a convent."

"Far fewer bruises there," said Erica.

"Yeah, but tough on the knees," said Dessie.

"Kenny's reasonably sane," Erica insisted. "Still, I imagine he's at home, practicing his brush strokes—"

"I would expect nothing less," Dessie finished.

"Well, hooray," said Erica. "Another one of the good guys makes it." She paused before her next question.

"And what about the multicultural casting for which the People's Theater is also famous?" Erica asked. "Last time I saw him, Kenny was very Caucasian. Will we be expanding our frame of reference for the inhabitants of Renaissance Italy?"

"Um, I don't know. Depends on who they think is right for the part," said Dessie uncertainly.

That sounds like a no, thought Erica. The People's core beliefs might not extend to this higher profile project.

"Oh, by the way, I saw Miranda on the way into rehearsal this morning," Erica offered, changing the subject. "She looks, um, good."

"Are you kidding?" said Dessie. "The face work is first rate, but her neck is still ringed like a sequoia."

"If we count the rings, will we know how old she is?" asked Erica.

"That could take a while," said Dessie. "How much time do you have?"

"Not enough," said Erica. "She did seem to have a whole lot of filler in her face. Insta-cheek, I call it. They all end up looking pretty much the same. I think there must be a law in LA that requires facial enhancement once you reach a certain age."

"Well, it is Miranda's last chance to get people to believe that she can play a character in the ballpark of thirty," said Dessie. "She'd better make the most of it. She's about ten years older than Kenny, who's playing her son as an adult."

"They married young in those days. But how do you know her age?" Erica asked.

"I counted the rings," said Dessie.

Shortly after Dessie uttered her previous remark, Miranda Owen made an unexpected entrance to the office. Dessie didn't miss a beat.

"Miranda," she began, "what a surprise."

"Always a pleasure, Dessie," Miranda replied, as air kisses were exchanged. "How have you been? It's been ages."

Miranda's tone was carefully calibrated to sound sincere but with a faint echo of the disingenuous. "Is Alex about?"

"Alex has not left the building," Dessie said, "but I don't know exactly where she is. Do you have time to wait?"

Dessie was no amateur at this game, and her tone suggested that it was her deepest hope that Miranda would not. Sadly, this was not to be.

Rather than taking a chair in the small waiting area near the coffee machine, or even making herself at home in Alex's office, Miranda chose to drape herself on Claudia's desk. Not on her chair but on her desk. Dessie looked stricken, and Miranda could not help but notice, looking down at the desk top on which she was sitting as if she had just become aware of where she was.

"Is this the desk?—oh, that poor dear." In saying this, Miranda betrayed about as much feeling as she would for the piece of lint that she flicked from her sleeve.

"Which poor dear?" asked Dessie, with acid in her tone. "The poor dear who died or the poor dear who got fired?"

"Someone got fired?" asked Miranda. "I hadn't heard. This place always was such a hotbed of activity."

"And you have always made it hotter," said Dessie.

"Well, how nice of you to say so," Miranda replied. "One does what one can." By now she had gotten off the desk and stood across from Dessie.

"As it happens, I can't wait," Miranda said, making a show of checking her watch. "Mustn't keep the director waiting. Bad form and all that. Unprofessional."

As she said this, Miranda opened the sleek leather shoulder bag that she had never relinquished, and in one continuous motion pulled out a pocket mirror and checked her make up.

"Well, if you gotta go," said Dessie. "Any message for Alex?"

"Just tell her I'd like a moment of her time. At her convenience, of course."

"Sure thing, Miranda. Oh, and Miranda," Dessie said, "I heard about how you handled the Bobby situation. May I say, good show."

Of all the things that had been said in the last few minutes, only this seemed genuine. For a moment, Miranda looked sincerely touched.

"Thanks, Dess," she said. "I appreciate that, coming from you."

"Well, you know I wouldn't say it if I didn't mean it."

"I do know that, Dessie," said Miranda. "So you'll tell Alex?"

"You know I will," Dessie replied, nodding to show her commitment.

"Bye, Dessie," said Miranda, as she flounced out of the room.

"Until the next time," Dessie said, returning to her desk.

Erica took this as her cue to find something to do behind her own desk. Having witnessed the entire exchange, Erica checked her card in Dessie's favor.

CHAPTER 20

"With what price we pay for the glory of motherhood."
Isadora Duncan

Later that afternoon, as Erica swung around the corner into Dessie's office, she was stopped short by what she saw there. Dessie was at her desk, as usual, but seated next to her, at Claudia's former post, was a girl, a much younger girl, who played with a stuffed bunny on her lap. The girl looked to be about eight, by Erica's unsure reckoning, and the boy who stood behind her, moving the swivel chair from side to side, was a year or two older. The boy's was a face she hadn't seen before, but the little girl was unmistakably her mother.

"Erica, hi," said Dessie. "You haven't met my children. This is Luke, and Claire."

Erica was pleasantly surprised to hear their names, fully expecting them to answer to Martin Jr. and Martine.

"Hi," Erica said. "Nice to meet you."

This was met by silence.

"Say hello to Erica," Dessie cautioned. "You don't mind if they call you Erica?" she asked.

"Not at all," Erica replied.

"Hi, Erica," said Luke, clearly the braver of the two. Claire simply took the bunny from her lap and placed it over her face.

"Claire . . ." Dessie began, drawing out the word.

"You know, sometimes I just feel like holding a bunny over my face," said Erica.

"Don't we all," agreed Dessie, smiling. "Okay, you two, I need to drop something over at Mr. Vartan's office," she said to her children. "Now remember what we talked about. Don't touch anything. Don't bother anybody. I'll be back in a minute."

As Dessie collected the papers on her desk, she quickly added, "I bet Erica wouldn't mind staying with you until I get back."

"Not at all," Erica repeated.

"Thanks," said Dessie. "Half days," she whispered to Erica. "They're the bane of my existence. What do teachers do on these so-called professional days?"

"Beats me," said Erica.

"But you were a teacher," said Dessie.

"We didn't have professional days. Or we did have them, every week. College classes don't meet every day. Usually, it's a two- or three-day schedule."

"With summers off?" asked Dessie.

"Yes, and most of January," said Erica.

"I've got to get me some of that," said Dessie. "For now I'd settle for a sitter who isn't sick."

"You're so on top of things, I'd expect you to have a back-up," said Erica.

"She's, um, unavailable," said Dessie, slightly stumbling over the answer. She quickly turned back to her children and added, "Remember what we talked about. If I get a good report from Erica, then maybe we can stop for ice cream on the way home."

Before leaving the room, Dessie grabbed her purse, which sat on the floor by her desk chair. She located her wallet and opened it, seemingly to check her cash supply for the proposed ice cream. Dessie pulled the bills from her wallet and quickly counted them. Her funds seemed to be sufficient, but her attention was elsewhere. As she replaced the bills, a folded sheet of beige paper slipped from her wallet and floated to the ground without her noticing. Erica did, however, but Dessie was on the move before she had a chance to point this out.

"Bribes," Dessie said, over her shoulder, to Erica. "A time-tested technique approved by mothers everywhere. Watch and learn, Erica. Watch and learn."

By now, Dessie was out the door. Erica planned to tell Dessie about the dropped paper upon her return, assuming it to be inconsequential, and turned her attention to the children. As she did, Alex came out of her office. She walked past Dessie's children without a break in her purposeful stride. Suddenly, she stopped herself and wheeled around.

"Luke, hello," she said. Before Luke could respond, Alex had moved on to his sister.

"Claire, is that you behind the bunny?"

"Yes," said a little voice, muffled by cotton stuffing.

"Nice bunny," Alex said, as she resumed her progress. "Erica," she said, nodding her greeting.

No time wasted on that, thought Erica. *Brisk, if not exactly cordial. Well, Alex has places to go, people to see. Apparently, little people, even Dessie's children, barely registered.*

The promise of ice cream still had not pried the bunny from Claire's face. Luke appeared to be the spokesman for the group. He was also the more fashion forward of the two, with his dark hair, gelled to within an inch of its life, pointing north. He dove right in.

"This is Claudia's chair," he began, maneuvering the desk chair from side to side as if handling a steering wheel. The weight of the little girl in the chair limited the range of motion and kept him from making any wide turns.

"Oh, you knew Claudia," said Erica, trying to sound neutral but more than a little surprised.

"Yes, she was nice. She used to come to our house and play with us. She was fun," said Luke. "And she made me this bracelet." He stuck out his right hand to show Erica an intricately beaded bracelet in varying shades of blue, held together by a shiny silver clasp.

Even Erica knew that if you tell a child not to talk about something, it immediately becomes Topic A.

"It's a boy's bracelet," Luke continued. "Like rock stars wear."

"It's cool," said Erica, recognizing the selection of beads she had seen in Claudia's apartment.

Claire chose this moment to join the conversation. Shifting her bunny to her right hand while still keeping the stuffed animal in front of her face, she held out her left. Wound around her wrist was a selection of pink beads stretched across an elastic thread. Claudia had wisely judged that Claire's fingers would not be able to handle the intricacy of a clasp, but a bracelet that stretched to fit would be just the thing.

"That's really pretty, Claire," said Erica. "Did Claudia make that for you?"

"Yes," said the voice behind the bunny. "She was fun." Claire then tilted her head backward, pointing her chin in the direction of her brother's voice. The bunny stayed in place. "Mommy said not to say," she warned.

"I know," said Luke to his sister. "It's kind of a secret," he said to Erica in a confidential tone.

Erica put her fingers to her lips and mimed turning the lock, in a gesture universally acknowledged as the promise to keep a secret. Her gesture must have emboldened Luke, who had something more to add:

"She went to heaven," he said, as if Claudia had headed off on vacation, with postcards expected, to be followed by gifts of souvenirs.

"Uh huh," said Erica, figuring that non-committal was the best way to go.

From behind the bunny, Claire was starting to lose patience. "Lukey, I'm starvating," she whimpered.

"It's *starving*, Claire," answered her brother. "And Mom said 'in a minute.'"

His sister replied with a theatrical sigh that Bernhardt would have admired.

By now, Dessie had come back to reclaim her children. In what appeared to be a single, fluid motion, she swept up her bag and her children, removed the bunny from her daughter's face, and bid Erica good bye before Erica had a chance to mention the piece of paper that had fallen to the floor.

"Thanks, Erica. See you tomorrow," Dessie said.

"Bye, bye," said Erica, waving as they passed her.

Dessie had her children out the door before Erica had time to give her report. It would have been thumbs up all around.

But before Erica returned to her desk, she went to the corner of the room where Dessie had dropped the piece of paper. Erica knew that the cleaning crew made their way to and through the offices on alternate Tuesdays, and only when the moon was full. Dessie's slip of paper could lie undisturbed for days. And while Erica assumed that the paper was nothing important, she would still do Dessie the courtesy of picking it up for her.

It was a small square, looking slightly weathered and showing the marks of having been folded for a very long time. Erica retrieved it and scanned the open page. It read:

I want to thank you for taking the baby. I know you will be good to her. Giving birth to her was the hardest thing I've ever done. I am going back to my life before. I have worked too hard to give it up now. It will be best for me and best for her. Thank you for the money. It will get me back to where I want to be, to the only life I have ever wanted.

It was the letter that Claudia's birth mother had sent to the Winthrops. The note that Claudia had copied into her journal and re-read countless times. The honest but dispassionate good bye that had stoked Claudia's anger and convinced her that her birth mother had to be destroyed by her avenging offspring. And Dessie carried it in her wallet.

Soon, Erica would carry it in hers.

CHAPTER 21

"It isn't all how *you* feel, it's what the play is doing. It isn't, "I
don't feel like doing this now," or, "I don't understand why I'm
doing this"—"Why, why, why?" None of your damn business,
that's what the playwright told you to do."
Jason Robards

After work that day, Erica had a question for Alan,
who had finished the acting portion of the film. Now,
he was on to looping, filling in the lines that could not
be salvaged from the production tracks. He had spent
the day re-recording dialogue by speaking his lines in
sync to "loops" of the visual image. The original
production track, which he heard through headphones,
served as his guide. Not only did he have to match the
wording and the lip movements, he also had to recreate
the nuance of the original performance. It's said that
Marlon Brando mumbled portions of his film
performances because he liked to loop. Given that the
emotional weight of a scene could shift with even a
slight adjustment to a few words or phrases, the
performance could not be frozen until the looping stage.
Alan didn't mumble, but on more than one occasion,
his performance competed with traffic noise, and the
sounds of the city usually won. It had been a long day,
but the looping was done.

"So how well did you all know each other, you
know, back in the day?" asked Erica.

"You make it sound like it was a hundred years
ago," said Alan, while moving on to his second glass of
wine. "I'm not that much older than you."

"Just enough to make it interesting," said Erica.

"Then, it's a loaded question," Alan ventured.

"Really, it's not," Erica insisted. "I'm just trying to figure out the chronology. I know you've known Dessie forever. How long is forever, by the way?"

"Well, let's see," Alan said. "Has it been twenty years? Maybe a little longer?"

"And Martin?" she asked.

"With Martin, it was longer. I used to see him at auditions. This was before he knew Dessie. Martin used to get around."

"Yes, I got that impression," Erica said.

"Yes, we all knew each other. You know who else was in the mix? The People's own Miranda Owen, before her recent television triumph. I haven't seen her in years, but I hear that she expects people to kneel before her, or maybe bow down to her bank account."

"You almost sound jealous," Erica said, enjoying it. "Until recently, I hadn't had the pleasure of seeing Miranda. In the flesh, as it were."

"Martin did," said Alan.

"Ooow," said Erica. "Do tell."

"She was in Martin's datebook," Alan confirmed.

"Along with most of the female population of New York, apparently," countered Erica.

"She was a more frequent visitor than most. And they were so happy for a time. Then Martin moved on, as he often did."

"Dessie knew that," said Erica. "She mentioned it when Miranda made her grand return to the stage."

"I don't know what Dessie knew and when she knew it," said Alan. "But I do know that meeting Dessie really changed Martin's life. I mean, he straightened up, as much as possible for him. They got married and they had two kids."

"So far, we have the American dream, actor style," said Erica. "And what about Alex?" she continued. "Was she part of the old gang?"

"She may have been around, but I didn't know her then. I know she's been at the People's Theater for a while, but she wasn't really on anyone's radar until *The Brothers Wittgenstein*. Then she was on everyone's radar."

"Yes, I would think that might make her the belle of the ball. But from what Dessie tells me, Alex doesn't go in for that sort of thing. With anyone or anything."

"I don't know," said Alan. "My meetings with Alex, although few and far between, have been strictly—"

"Let me guess," said Erica. "Professional."

"How did you know?" asked Alan.

"I've met her, haven't I?" asked Erica. "For Alex, it's all about the professional. The personal, not so much. I saw her walk by Dessie's kids today as if they were inanimate objects. Although she did manage to squeeze out a hello."

"Well, not everyone has the maternal gene, now do they?" asked Alan, pointedly. Erica seemed not to hear and continued with her own train of thought.

"And I heard the strangest thing today. Dessie adores those children, but on more than one occasion, she left them in the care of Claudia, the girl who is, sadly, dead, but was definitely incompetent."

"That news doesn't exactly knock me off my seat," Alan replied.

"This is Dessie we're talking about, Alan. She acted as though she wouldn't leave a puppy she liked in Claudia's care, but she let Claudia take care of her children?"

"What's the big deal? From what little I know of this," he said, "if it means a night out, most parents will go for the fourteen year old who can more or less make eye contact."

"But this wasn't once," Erica argued. "It was on a regular basis. Dessie opened her home to this girl."

"Maybe Claudia was great with kids," Alan said.

"I still can't see Dessie risking her kids' safety with a babysitter of questionable ability. Next to the departed Martin, her kids are everything to Dessie."

"Still not convinced," said Alan. "And how did you come by this earthshaking news?"

"The kids spilled the beans, or maybe I should say, the beads," Erica began.

"Or maybe you shouldn't," Alan said.

"Claudia had made these bracelets for the kids, which they showed me. Really lovely work. I know they were hers because I recognized the patterns from my trip to Claudia's apartment."

"The less said about that visit, the better," Alan began, before asking, "and how did you know for sure that Claudia was the one who made them?"

"I saw a few samples in the apartment. All meticulous, and very distinctive patterns."

"Small world, the world of beads," Alan said.

"Small enough," said Erica. "It's just that this wasn't a snapshot I expected to see in Dessie's family album. But let's move on to more important business. Dinner?"

"I vote yes," Alan replied.

"Well, you look like you've had a hard day," said Erica.

"So, you'll cook?" he asked, surprised.

"No, of course not," she said. "But I'll let you choose."

"I have choices?" he said.

"Of course," she answered. "Take out or eat out."

"Are there any other choices?" asked Alan.

"Not that I know of," Erica said. "So it is . . . ?"

"Eat out," he said after thinking for a moment.
"Good answer," Erica replied.

CHAPTER 22

"They are not all made to be mothers."
Henrik Ibsen, from his Notes for *Hedda Gabler*

"I saw the strangest thing on my way in today," said Erica to Dessie when she saw her the next morning.

"What, pray tell?" asked Dessie.

"Well, in the subway, I saw two little kids, a boy and a girl, practicing on their violins."

"I've seen that a number of times," said Dessie. "It seems like a good place to practice. They don't really bother anybody, and they might make some coin in the process."

"I don't know how well these two were going to do. Their mother was there, filming them. They were real beginners, scratching away. But that wasn't the weird part."

"Erica, parents film their children doing everything, from the moment they come out of the womb. They even film that," Dessie said. "You should get out more."

"No, it was the way the mother held the camera," Erica insisted. "Like a gun she was pointing at them. And that's the way the kids reacted. They were scared."

"That is a little more troubling. How old did these kids look?" Dessie asked.

"About the same age as your two," Erica answered.

"I wonder why they weren't in school," Dessie said.

"I wasn't about to confront her," Erica replied. "She had a video camera and she wasn't afraid to use it."

Dessie offered a slight smile in response to Erica's last remark.

"Your kids are great, by the way," Erica continued. "It was so nice to meet them."

"Thanks," said Dessie, trying not to look as pleased as she was. "I hope they behaved while I was gone."

"It was only a couple of minutes," said Erica. "They were fine."

"What did you find to talk about?" asked Dessie, showing not a hint of concern.

"Well, I don't know much, but I do know that with kids, their interests are your interests, or it's going to be a very short conversation. We talked about bunnies. I admired their bead bracelets. That was pretty much it."

Dessie's eyes narrowed at the mention of the bracelets, but Erica could hold her own in giving nothing away.

"They seem like happy, healthy kids, Dessie. You should be very proud."

Dessie visibly relaxed as her maternal pride, like a powerful drug, took effect.

"I am," she said, "very proud. They do look good, which is surprising, considering that I have nursed them through every childhood disease known to the medical community, and a few known only to veterinary science."

"Nothing too serious?"

Seeing Erica's evident concern, Dessie relieved it. "Just the standard-issue childhood ailments, with maybe a few embellishments. Then there's all the school activities. For the past two years, I've been president of the PTA, although I'm happy to say that I just passed the crown to another PTA mother."

"With the end of your reign, does that make you PTA Queen Mother?" Erica asked.

"I'd have to think about that," said Dessie. "This motherhood thing is a lot of work, however you slice it. Much more when you do it alone."

"I'm sure," Erica agreed. "Who takes care of them during the day, when you're here?" she ventured.

"I knew a lot of out-of-work actors when the kids were very little," said Dessie. "They filled in when I was working. I still know a lot of out-of-work actors," she admitted, "but now the kids are in school. I drop them off in the morning, and I have a woman—she's not in theater, as it happens—who picks them up after school, makes dinner, and stays until I get home. Unless she gets sick, of course."

"Yes, you said something about a back-up," began Erica.

"I'm looking for a replacement," said Dessie briskly, before changing the subject. "I love to talk about my kids, but we've got to keep moving. We have a lot to do this morning."

"Whatever you say, Dessie," answered Erica, as she watched the window of opportunity closing. "What's on the agenda?" she asked. "And before I forget, please send my best to Claire and Luke." *Whom I like even better,* Erica thought. *Obviously, these kids can keep a secret. Well, some secrets.*

Just like Erica.

CHAPTER 23

"Acting is merely the art of keeping a large group of people from
coughing."
Ralph Richardson

"You're home late," said Alan, looking up from the
sofa on which he reclined. The television, turned down
low, was a mild hum in the background.

"I was advancing the cause of American Theater in
the twenty-first century," said Erica. "By sitting
through one of the worst plays written in the twenty-
first century."

"Don't you think you're getting ahead of yourself?"
asked Alan.

"Check back with me in 2075," said Erica. "I doubt I
will have changed my opinion."

"And the play?" Alan inquired.

"Oh, you mean, the thing?" replied Erica. "It was
'the love that dare not speak its name' screaming in
your face for two hours. The type of play Joe Orton
would have written after they took a hammer to his
head."

"Don't hold back," said Alan. "Tell me what you
really think."

"I think it was better than the caveman play I saw
last week. Where they grunted at us for ninety
minutes."

"Then why didn't you leave?" Alan wanted to know.

"As I said, ninety minutes. No intermission. Very
clever on their part."

"No, I mean tonight's offering. I'm assuming that the bad Orton had an intermission."

"Yes, in fact, it did," said Erica. "A calculated risk on the part of the production team. I expected a stampede of enraged theatergoers."

"So why didn't you leave?" Alan asked.

"Because," said Erica. "It isn't done at the People's Theater. Free tickets for the worker bees are a major perk. It would be a violation of our ethic to leave: The People's people sit it out. I have seen them flipping through magazines during the entire second act, dim lights and all, and that's okay. But you don't walk out."

"There was one fun bit," she continued. "A phone rang about half way through the second act."

"That was the fun bit?" asked Alan, incredulous.

"Not usually," Erica replied. "If I had a phone that went off during a performance, I would be mortified. In fact, I think the word *mortified* exists for just such occasions."

"I don't disagree," said Alan. "Was the alleged offender mortified?"

"Yes," Erica answered. "To her credit. It was not a very big theater, so the culprit was easy to identify. In case there were any doubt, she began to paw through a seemingly bottomless purse, searching for the phone. It kept ringing and ringing, and she kept digging and digging . . ."

"Don't they stop ringing at a point?"

"They're supposed to," Erica answered. "But it seemed to go on forever. She must have set it for about 27 rings before the recorded message kicks in. And, as I said, it was a small theater, so this was not lost on the actors."

"Did someone speak to her? Or did one of the actors address her from the stage? I've heard of that happening," Alan volunteered.

"Actually, no." said Erica. "*Better*. First, the actor who was the furthest downstage came all the way to the edge of the stage and stared at her. He was followed, one by one, by the rest of the cast, at least the ones who were on the stage at the time. And pretty much the whole cast was onstage at the time. They just stood there, staring at her. And the harder they stared, the harder a time she had finding the phone and shutting it off. Maybe shutting it up is closer to the truth. We were at a tense moment in the play when the ringing began— of course—so any antagonism the characters, or the actors, were feeling worked for this particular moment. No one had to break character."

"Her fingers, maybe," said Alan. "Character, never."

"Tell me how you really feel," Erica began.

"Just so we're clear," Alan replied.

"As a bell," said Erica. "Or the ringer on a phone."

"What happened in the end?"

"Well," Erica answered. "She finally found the still ringing phone. She grabbed it, said a quick 'I can't talk,' and reburied it in her bag, presumably hitting the off button as it made its way down. The rest of the audience, which had been watching, spellbound, exploded in laughter, which may have helped relieve some of the tension they were feeling as they watched the play. This play had no laughs, as I think you can guess. At least, none that were intentional. A cathartic groan was more what the playwright had in mind, and the actors were on the same page. So, as a group, the actors shifted their gaze from the offending theatergoer to the rest of us, staring us down until the laughter stopped. Which it did, and quickly. Then off they went with the rest of the play, followed by tepid applause at the curtain call."

"Do you think it was staged?" Alan asked skeptically. "One of those spontaneous moments that happens eight times a week?

"I don't think so," said Erica. "If it was, sign that girl up. She's a Keaton in the making. Diane, by way of Buster."

"And on the other side of the footlights?" Alan ventured.

"I'm beginning to think that very little happens at the People's Theater that's not preplanned, pre-rehearsed, and otherwise staged for the benefit of the audience, whoever that audience might be," said Erica.

"Including you," said Alan.

"I seem to have VIP seating," Erica said.

"So it would seem. How do you think the play will do?" Alan asked.

"I won't say the worst reviews since John Wilkes Booth," she replied, "but in that general vicinity. And you're welcome to join me next time," she added. "I get two tickets per show."

"You make it sound so tempting," said Alan.

"I do, don't I?" said Erica, joining him in a prone position on the sofa. "Don't even try. Resistance is futile."

CHAPTER 24

"The wind that blows
Is all that anybody knows."
                    Henry David Thoreau

Erica returned from lunch the next day with the expectation of an easy rest of the afternoon. Dessie would be out—one of her rare absences—with plans to attend a school play in which Luke was making his theatrical debut. Luke's school performed only matinees, which made it tricky for working parents with a less-than-understanding boss. But Dessie was the boss for all intents and purposes, and off she went. Erica planned to spend the afternoon hidden in her office, working on her current research interests— Michelangelo and the adoptions laws in Maine—and these would keep her busy until quitting time.

But the best laid plans have a habit of unraveling. As Erica approached the theater, she saw on the sidewalk none other than Jenn, the indefatigable production assistant from the film project that had previously occupied Alan. Oblivious to the world around her, Jenn was texting with an aggression usually reserved for debutante balls. She took no notice of Erica, who slipped into the theater through the side door and quickly made her way to the office.

Climbing the stairs, she passed a couple, a male and a female, who were deep in conversation. They were also clearly pro-piercing, given the amount of metal each wore to decorate any number of orifices.

"Did you hear? Alan DeLorme is in the building," she sighed.

"Oh, I love him," he answered.

"Yeah, me too," said Erica, whose presence on the stairs surprised them.

"Me too, totally," the female replied, as she ran a hand through her tousled mane as if to say that in a standoff, Erica would have a hard time holding her own. This gesture might have been more convincing if her thick head of wavy hair had been one color rather than many, and if none of the colors were puce. But her point seemingly made, the pair and Erica quickly parted.

Outside her office, in the reception area with the coffee maker that no longer served up Claudia's dubious brew, Erica was treated to the rare sight of Dessie being hugged, lifted, in fact, off the floor, by a male figure, a figure Erica knew only too well. The tiny woman nearly lost her clogs as Alan spun her around while Dessie's laughter echoed up and down the hallway. Although Dessie had a sense of humor—she would have to, given the life she'd been handed—Erica had never seen her so light-hearted. Alan gently placed Dessie on the ground just as Erica was nearing the couple.

"Well, it looks like Old Home Week," said Erica as she entered the room. "You should have told me," she said directly to Alan.

"I didn't know myself," he replied.

"What a surprise!" said Dessie. "Well, I'll leave you two. I have to go watch my son steal the show. Always a pleasure, Alan," she said, patting him on the arm. "Don't be such a stranger." Dessie turned and walked in the direction of the door, her step markedly more buoyant. "Oh, and Erica," she said, "I left some files on your desk. Will you go through them to make sure they're all in order? We have a few people who are due for a personnel review."

"Not me, I hope," Erica said.

"A pleasure yet to come," replied Dessie, as she sailed out the door.

"See you, Dess," said Alan. He then turned to Erica.

"Is there somewhere we could talk?" he asked.

"Always," Erica answered. "But not here," she said, indicating her office with a tilt of her head. "Let's take a walk."

Erica quickly led Alan in the direction of one of the more obscure outposts of the People's Theater, a sitting area that had once served as a dressing room until the small theater adjoining it had been expanded. A new performance space—which Dessie hoped to name after her late husband Martin—would take its place. For the time being, it served no particular purpose beyond giving Erica a place to take a breath when her trips to the library became suspiciously frequent. Following a few back hallways to their destination allowed Alan to travel virtually incognito in the one building in which he could be recognized as a celebrity.

"So, hi there," Erica began, when they had settled themselves on a pair of well worn chairs that faced each other. "Why didn't you mention you were coming by?" she asked, smiling, but with a slight strain in her voice.

"I didn't know," said Alan.

"I saw your stalker outside. She looks well," Erica continued. "Is she here for you?"

"Yes and no," said Alan.

"There's at least fifty percent of that answer I don't like," Erica said.

"Let me explain," Alan offered.

"No one's stopping you," said Erica, trying and failing to sound gracious.

"You're not going to believe this—"

"Try me," she said calmly.

"Okay, here it is," he began. "The director wants to shoot some additional scenes—"

"Is that all?" replied Erica, sounding dismayed. "Then why make such a big deal about it? A simple phone call would have sufficed."

"This takes more than a phone call. He wants to shoot the scenes in Prague. I'm flying there tonight."

"You're what!"

"Flying to Prague. Tonight. My bags are packed. I'm ready to go."

"How in the world did they find the money to shoot extra scenes? In Prague, no less."

"I don't know," said Alan. "I'm not the money man. It's just a short trip—five days, maybe—"

"But transporting all those people? Couldn't they find a corner of New York, or maybe even Vancouver, that looks enough like Prague to keep the director happy?"

"Well, I think he's going for the real sights and sounds. There's an 1100-year-old castle in a place called Matrika Praha—"

"Matrika what?" asked Erica, still in disbelief.

"Matrika Praha. It means 'little Prague.' And there are some beautiful views from the bridges on the Vltava River," Alan chattered on. "I assume we'll be parking ourselves in some picturesque spot."

"How did you get to be an expert, all of a sudden?" Erica asked.

"Oh, Jenn had some research materials in the car," replied Alan.

"Now we're getting somewhere," snapped Erica. "Are you going to Prague with Jenn?"

"No, I'm going to the airport with Jenn," Alan answered. "When she drops me curbside at Kennedy, then her connection to the film ends."

"What about her connection to you?" asked Erica.

"She has no connection to me," Alan insisted, "and more to the point, I have no connection to her—beyond hoping she's a better driver on the highway than she is in the city. So, if we make it safely to Kennedy, it's a hearty farewell and Jenn finds a new job. I think she may already have something lined up," Alan finished.

"Don't be surprised when you open your luggage and find her stowed inside," said Erica.

"She'd have to be a contortionist to make it into my carry on," Alan offered.

"I wouldn't put it past her," Erica replied. "And will the Czech equivalent of Jenn be meeting you in Prague?" she asked.

"Actually, I requested a burly teamster," said Alan.

"Male or female?" asked Erica.

"I'm not picky," Alan answered. "And while I find this hint of jealousy oddly appealing, I think you should know it's a waste of time." He checked his watch. "And I don't have much to spare. So can we say our good byes before I brave the Long Island Expressway with Jenn at the wheel?"

"You might want to sit in the back," Erica warned. "It's probably safer. And remind her to keep her hands on the wheel."

"Both of them," said Alan. "At all times."

"And no email or Twitter," Erica said. "I saw her going at it on the sidewalk. She's scary when she's texting."

"I won't even let her listen to music," Alan added, as he stood up. "Instead, I'll hum the whole way there."

"That sounds like punishment enough. Yes, I am satisfied," said Erica, rising to meet him.

"That's all that matters, then," Alan said, as he leaned in to envelop her in his arms. "I promise to be in frequent contact. And it's only for a couple of days. The money and the producer's patience can't last forever. I should be back in less than a week."

"Okay, then," Erica answered, with a trace of resistance left in her voice.

"So what can I bring you back?" he asked after relinquishing his hold on her.

"The cheesiest trinket you can find in beautiful downtown Prague," she began. "And yourself. Not necessarily in that order."

"You got it," he said, before offering her a kiss, which she accepted. "Gotta go."

"I know," she said quietly.

Alan smiled at her. "Zitje blaze," he said.

"What?" Erica asked.

"It's 'good bye' in the Czech Republic," Alan proudly answered.

"Now you're scaring me," she said. "Please don't tell me that Jenn looked it up for you."

"She didn't," said Alan, a little hurt. "I looked it up myself. Just like a big boy."

"Well, I'm truly touched," Erica replied, trying to sound as if she meant it. "And I will miss you," she insisted, "even if it's only for five days."

"That's what we like to hear," Alan said. "Even if it's only for five days."

When Alan began to move in the direction that they had come, Erica offered an alternative. "I'll show you a quicker way out. That way, you can avoid some of the more eager members of your fan base, most of whom seem to work in this building. But once you hit the street, you're on your own."

"I think I can manage," Alan said, as she led him to the back exit of the theater, which led to the alley that led to the street. Alan looked skeptical as she opened the door that abutted the dumpster.

"I'm sorry to have to say good bye with the smell of garbage in the air," Alan began. "But I'll see you soon." With a quick kiss, he exited.

Erica watched as he picked his way down the alley, avoiding the pieces of debris that had been abandoned in places near and around the dumpster. It took him a few minutes to reach the street, and then he was gone. Erica looked down the empty alley for a minute or two, then closed the door and prepared to return to work. She had only one thing to declare—out loud but to herself.

"You're going to Prague?" she said, which was quickly followed by, "Actually, just as well."

Erica returned to her desk, to the task that Dessie had left for her. She has no idea what she was supposed to be looking for, but expected there would be an answer in the files.

The three folders belonged to Asha and Chloe, and squeezed between them, the first time anything had come between them as far as Erica knew, was Claudia. Either the People's Theater had a stricter policy than most, holding the deceased accountable for their actions, or Claudia's file did not belong in this pile. Dutifully, Erica opened the files and read.

Asha and Chloe had unsurprising stories. Both resided on the Upper East Side, within blocks of each other. Both had graduated from an impressive array of ivy-covered schools, followed by internships with the biggest names on Broadway. Greatness, no doubt, would be thrust upon them.

Claudia, on the other hand, had a less usual tale to tell. A high school graduate, she had worked most recently as a checker at a supermarket, with previous training at a 7-11. Erica had already heard Claudia's story, but her file held one unusual detail that both Asha and Chloe's lacked. Folded neatly in thirds was a copy of her birth certificate, the one listing her parents as Ray and Etta Winthrop. Perhaps confirmation was needed that Claudia actually existed. But here was the ticket to Claudia's true identity and Erica's chance to commit fraud. All she needed was a notarized copy of the application for the original birth certificate. Erica knew she could fill out the form, but how would she get it notarized, without proof positive that she was Claudia? She could get a money order for the fee, but would the state of Maine accept an application from the recently deceased? Would the office of birth records know what the office of deaths had recently registered?

Given that Dessie had failed to include instructions as to what a personnel review entailed, Erica replaced the files on Dessie's desk without comment. She then returned to her own desk and did something she should have done a long time ago.

She googled Dessie.

From the vast resources available online, Erica quickly learned that Dessie had not exaggerated her acting career. While Dessie's acting days were an increasingly distant but still vivid memory, the proof of what might have been could be found in reviews of productions that ran in basement theaters, fringe festivals, and the occasional theatrical venue where the audience was not treated to the sound of the single toilet flushing at a critical juncture. Dessie was variously described as a compelling Nora in *Doll's House*, a comic yet forthright Lina Szczepanowska, the acrobatic aviatrix in Shaw's *Misalliance*, and, most poignantly, as a Hermione in Shakespeare's *The Winter's Tale* who brought the audience and the critic to tears when her lost daughter was restored to her. Dessie's acting range was impressive, but even more surprising was a talent she had displayed earlier in her career.

She played basketball.

On her high school basketball team, Dessie ran the offense in the position of point guard. The point guard is usually the shortest and often the fastest member of the team, the one who runs the show, controlling the game by making sure that the right player gets the ball at the right time. Calling the plays was a habit Dessie had developed early in life.

Dessie's success as a point guard was aided and abetted by her teammate, the shooting guard, a player who is usually taller than the point guard—which wouldn't be hard, in this case. More importantly, the shooting guard creates a shot for herself or finds someone else who is open, so that another player can have a shot at the basket. The shooting guard creates as many shots as possible, finding the available talent and using it to the best of its ability.

Old habits die hard, thought Erica.

Described as "the long and the short of it" by an enterprising sports writer, the point guard and the shooting guard had been teammates for all four years in high school, inseparable on the court and off. One year, they even led their team, the Portersville Spuds, to the division finals. These achievements were impressive, given that Portersville High fielded a team from the population of a small farming community. The "long" of the dynamic duo was five feet, seven inches tall, hardly a giantess, but among the tallest on the team. Their triumph might have ended in a crowded gymnasium in the late 1980's were it not for the fact that the reunion committee of Portersville High, Class of '89, had sent out word, online of course, when their twentieth reunion was on the horizon, and they wanted EVERYONE to be there. The committee had posted a series of "Remember When's," complete with pictures of the days they would never forget. Who could forget the time that the women's basketball team went to the big game in Bangor, led by Ally and Dess, the long and the short of it? Both had gone off to make it big in the theater. At least one of them did. Dessie's partner in crime had been one Ally Wallace, like Dessie, a girl from a small town in Maine.

"Ally Wallace," said Erica to herself, as she turned off her computer for the day. "It doesn't exactly roll off the tongue."

At home that evening, Erica had plenty of time to contemplate the question before her without interruption or interrogation. Her interest was not in sports history but birth history. Claudia had deliberately found her way into the People's Theater in search of her condemned mother. She had found out the identity of her birth mother. Now Erica would try to do the same, keeping in mind that finding the birth mother didn't necessarily mean she had found Claudia's killer.

Erica's task should have been made easier by the fact that most of the People's people were the same age as Claudia. Many were younger. Many were men. In fact, the pickings were pretty slim. Flouncing her way in and out of rooms, Miranda Owen may have been able to play a mother, but she seemed unlikely to live the part, given that her chief interest in life was herself. Suzie Q walked with a steadier tread, but she had her own surprising and unexpected family. Both women were the right age, but neither seemed to be in the running. In fact, anyone involved in *Michelangelo* was probably off the hook due to the fact that Claudia's arrival at the theater predated Michelangelo's. But both Miranda and Suzie went way back with the People's Theater, and there was no telling what had happened in their distant past to make them the women they had become. Either one could have given up a child for adoption, leading to Miranda's self-absorption and

Suzie's unwavering devotion to her duties, both maternal and professional. Still, Claudia would have had no idea about the production, which was announced about six months after her arrival, much less who would be in the cast and on the crew.

So it was likelier to be someone who was already ensconced at the People's Theater. Now the pickings were even slimmer. Alex seemed an unlikely choice, given her complete investment in the People's Theater and her total lack of interest in anyone or anything not on the production schedule. Dessie, on the other hand, lived for her children, organizing her life around their continued well being. Regardless of the circumstances, whatever they might be, it seemed unlikely that she would leave a child of hers behind. At the same time, like Suzie, a lost child might have enhanced Dessie's devotion to her maternal duty. So that left . . . no one, as far as Erica knew, to add to the pool of potential parents. Erica also knew that learning the identity of Claudia's birth mother would get her that much closer to her murderer, and that they could well be one and the same.

CHAPTER 25

"You walk in, plant yourself squarely on both feet, look the other
fella in the eye, and tell the truth."
James Cagney

It was a Monday night—a non-show night—so the lobby once again stood empty. Erica was reasonably sure they were the only people left in the building. She and Dessie had been working in Dessie's office all afternoon and into the evening on the reorganization of the theater's filing system. The People's Theater was cutting edge when it came to the plays produced and the technology used to produce them. Projected scenery, rather than the clunky three-dimensional kind, had become *de rigeur*, to the point where the pyrotechnics sometimes upstaged the show, leaving it stranded in the rocket's red glare. No one called the lighting cues anymore: that task had been farmed out to a computer that never complained about the pay. But when it came to the offstage technology, the People's Theater had a long way to go. Information that should have been available online was not; instead, filing cabinets could be found in a variety of locations, all stuffed with papers, some trivial, some essential. If the offstage technology found its equivalent onstage, the shows would be lit by gaslight.

It had taken weeks to finish the task, but Dessie and Erica had come up with a system that would require most of the army of the ambitious, who had left the building at least an hour ago, to spend the next few weeks transcribing the material into online files. They had no idea what they were in for. Then again, neither did Dessie.

Erica wanted to finish this task, her small contribution, before she and Dessie sat down for a little talk. Now it was done. And now it was time. Erica wasn't sure how Dessie would react to what she had to say, but she knew she had to say it.

"Good work, Erica," Dessie said. "This seemed to take forever, but I think we can be very proud of ourselves. It will change the way the information flows around here. I won't go as far as to say revolutionize, but it will certainly speed things up. Now we can find things without sending out a search team."

"Always at your service," said Erica. "Always have been," she added. "But that was the idea, wasn't it?"

"What do you mean?" said Dessie, still poring over the plan for the filing system that lay open on her desk.

"Where are the kids tonight?" Erica asked. "Who's staying with them?"

"Um, they're with the regular sitter," replied Dessie, still distracted by the task at hand.

"I guess you didn't need the standby after all," Erica said.

"No, not really," replied Dessie, finally giving her full attention to Erica. "Why do you ask?"

"I guess she was no Claudia," said Erica.

"She—what?" asked Dessie.

"Why did you do it, Dessie?"

"Why did I?—oh, you mean, let Claudia take care of the kids?" Dessie laughed lightly. "Okay, I admit it. I let her take care of my kids once in a while. She needed the money. Sometimes, I needed the help. She certainly did better with children than she did with adults. And the kids liked her."

Dessie paused before adding, "I don't know why, but they just seemed to get each other, Claudia and my kids. I never understood it. Now maybe I'm disqualified for Mother of the Year, but no harm was done. Everyone survived."

"Almost everyone," said Erica.

"What do you mean?" Dessie asked, with a slight furrow of her brow.

"Claudia was a regular visitor to your apartment, wasn't she?" said Erica. "She wasn't just a sometime babysitter. I wouldn't say you adopted her," she continued, while checking Dessie's reaction, "but she came by a lot."

Dessie responded with a long intake of breath, which she let out with a sigh.

"And, no, your children didn't give the game away," Erica reassured her. "You've trained them well. But they did talk about Claudia, and they did show me the bracelets they're both so proud of."

"Those are nice bracelets," said Dessie. "The kids love them. They won't take them off. And I don't see why they should have to."

"Nor do I," said Erica. "Claudia did beautiful work. But she wouldn't have gone to that kind of trouble for children she knew only casually. Those pieces took a lot of time. More than almost anything she did, they show a lot of feeling. Claudia obviously cared about your kids. And they cared about her."

"They're great kids," said Dessie in a faraway voice that matched the look in her eyes. But Erica was still there, still in the present.

"You took her in, Dessie. You took her into your home. Maybe not into your trust."

Dessie visibly shook herself and returned to the conversation, even as she tried to shake Erica off.

"So she took care of my kids. So she made them bracelets. So what?" asked Dessie.

Erica tacked in a different direction. "You know what I like about you, Dessie. You always tell the truth. It's just that it's always on a slant."

"What's that supposed to mean?"

"Why did you send me to Claudia's apartment?" Erica demanded.

"To do as I asked," replied Dessie. "To send a few things to Claudia's family."

"Not to find anything?" asked Erica.

"What did you have in mind?"

"How about Claudia's journal? Volume Two? You remember, the Adoption Search Years."

"Well, you did find me Volume One," Dessie said without a trace of emotion.

"I did at that," said Erica. "And I dutifully turned it over to you. But somehow it landed in the trash."

Dessie's surprise was evident. "Don't worry, Dessie, I retrieved it," Erica said. "Ever dutiful. And I'm keeping it safe."

"Okay," said Dessie cautiously.

"So you knew there was a Volume Two," Erica began.

"So you say," answered Dessie, gingerly.

"Yes, there's a sequel," Erica confirmed. "A real page turner. Let me summarize the plot. You remember the mother she was so angry with in Part One? The one who gave birth to her and then gave her away? Or maybe sold her for a small commission? I'm not talking a million-dollar settlement. But enough to get Mom back on her feet and back to the bright lights of Broadway."

"I'm listening," said Dessie.

"But I want *you* to talk, Dessie. You still haven't explained why you sent me to Claudia's apartment."

"Why don't you do it," said Dessie coolly.

"As ever, your wish is my command," Erica replied. "You sent me to Claudia's apartment hoping I would find something. Nothing too incriminating. At least nothing that incriminated you."

"What are you saying, Erica?" asked Dessie.

"You knew there was nothing to find in her apartment. Seeing to the details, as always. I would say 'cleaning up,' but you did leave the place a mess."

"And when was this exactly?" asked Dessie, still under control.

"Oh, didn't I say?" answered Erica, matching her. "It was the night you killed Claudia."

Dessie's face registered shock and surprise, but she quickly recovered.

"Erica, have you been lying in wait all day to spring this nonsense on me? Or are you just lying? Unfounded accusations can get you into a lot of trouble, you know, serious trouble. And if this is your idea of a joke, no one thinks it's funny."

Dessie had drawn herself up to her almost five feet in stature and stood face to face with Erica, Dessie's being the face that was looking up. With arms akimbo, she stood in a pose borrowed from Superman, or possibly Mighty Mouse.

"Dessie, are you threatening me?" Erica asked.

"Well, you seem to be threatening me," Dessie replied, "and I don't take well to threats."

As Erica looked away for a moment, she felt a small fist connect with her chin at just the right angle to send her spinning, like a bewildered dancer who had missed the beat. Unable to stop herself, she hit the floor, and when she looked up, she saw Dessie standing over her, a small revolver having replaced the small fist.

"Dessie, is that a gun?" Erica asked, incredulous.

"It is," Dessie calmly replied.

"Where in the world did you get a gun?" Erica wanted to know.

"Prop table," said Dessie crisply. "From *Titus Andronicus*. A modern production set in an open-carry state."

"Oh, so it's a fake gun with fake bullets," Erica said. "Just to scare me."

"I wouldn't test that theory if I were you," answered Dessie. "It could be a real gun with fake bullets. We go for authenticity at the People's Theater. Or it could be a real gun with real bullets. You don't think I could get real bullets?"

"I would never doubt you, Dessie. I will take it on trust that you have the upper hand here. But could I at least get off the floor?"

"Erica, you may get up and sit quietly in a chair," Dessie said. "Sit in Claudia's chair. Now be a good girl because this gun is trained on you and only you," Dessie continued, as she watched Erica make the slow and careful transition from the floor to the chair that Dessie indicated.

"And you just happened to have a gun in your purse for what, special occasions?" asked Erica once she was seated. "I hope you don't plan to keep it at home."

"Of course not," said Dessie, shocked at the suggestion. "I would never leave a gun anywhere near the kids."

"And the *Titus* people won't miss it?" asked Erica.

"They might," said Dessie. "Or I may get it back to the prop table before tomorrow's rehearsal. Depends on how things go here with you."

Erica had not expected things to escalate to violence, and she was pretty sure that, minus the gun, she could take the diminutive Dessie. But with no desire to get into a wrestling match with an armed assailant, Erica also knew that she needed to calm things down, and in a hurry. And the best way to do that was to appeal to the actor in Dessie. Her only hope was to keep Dessie occupied by giving her the center stage that she craved, to keep her talking until Erica came up with a way out of this, or, on the off chance that help might arrive in some way, shape, or form. And Erica was not picky. Any way, shape, or form would do.

"Dessie, you know that what I'm saying is the truth," Erica began.

"I expect that no one knows that but you," answered Dessie, who had backed into her own chair with the gun still pointing at Erica. Once seated, she visibly relaxed.

"You're a far more creative type than you let on, Erica. Such an imagination. Does Alan know what he has in you? But we really can't have you making ridiculous accusations. In the first place, they can be harmful. To me, to the People's Theater. Not to mention to you, and possibly even to Alan's career. You never know where things might go if you start making baseless, maybe even slanderous, statements."

Erica said nothing, waiting to see how far Dessie would take this.

"And what proof do you have?" Dessie continued. "From what Alex has told me, there were no relevant finger prints. They have no clues. Claudia had no known enemies. No particular friends. She was a tabloid headline for about a day and a half, and then people moved on to the next dead girl. What is there left to say, or to do, for that matter?"

Erica felt a trickle of sweat working its way down her back, and was grateful that it was out of Dessie's sightline. She needed more than anything to keep the conversation on the level of business as usual. Just an amiable chat between two co-workers, despite the fact that one of them was packing heat.

"Yes, Dessie, you were in an enviable position," Erica said. "How better to keep tabs than by sitting at the right hand—or was it the right ear?—of the person with the most information. Alex kept you up to date on everything that was happening—or not happening—in the investigation."

"Erica, much as I enjoy chatting with you, I do not intend to listen to much more of this. And I have to get home to my children. So let's make this short and sweet." Dessie took a deep breath and began.

"I'm saying this only because there's no one here but us, and I know you lack the skill to be taping our conversation. I can tell from the look on your face that you didn't think of it. And if you repeat any part of this, I'll deny every word of it tomorrow."

Dessie took another deep breath and continued.

"Yes, I killed her. It wasn't planned. It just happened. Claudia and I had stayed late in the office, on a night like this, come to think of it. Just she and I, just like you and I here tonight. Claudia had finished up her work much earlier in the afternoon, from what I could tell. She was still at her desk, and her desk was its usual mess. But for some reason, she seemed pleased about something. As if she had come to a decision.

"I made a final trip to the ladies room before taking the long subway ride home. When I got back, Claudia was not at her desk, but her things were there. That giant sack she carried around was still in her desk drawer. Or half falling out of it. I saw the light on in Alex's office, but she had left for a board meeting uptown hours earlier. When I went in, Claudia was standing over the awards case. It was unlocked, as we all now know. Claudia had taken out the Kemby, the one for *The Brothers Wittgenstein*. She was holding it over her head, waving it. Then she started dancing around. Like a sprite in front of a bonfire. Dancing with a freedom I never imagined she had."

"Must have been quite a sight," said Erica, still eyeing Dessie's gun.

"I'll never forget it," Dessie said curtly. "When she turned around and saw me, that was the end of the dancing. Then she started spewing threats. She said that this award belonged to her, that she had been traded for it. She kept repeating that she had been sold, traded her for a Kemby, and once the word got out, it would bring down the theater. She said I could say good bye to naming the new theater after Martin. All I could think was that this cannot happen."

"Dessie, couldn't you have just separated her from the Kemby?" Erica asked. "If she's alive, she's a disturbed and angry girl, venting her frustrations. If she's dead, well, you've got a dead girl on your hands." Erica paused for a moment.

"And while we're at it, Dessie, we don't live in a Victorian novel. Children are born out of wedlock all the time. Currently, it's in vogue among certain starlets. No one's life is automatically ruined."

"I didn't stop to think. I couldn't," Dessie answered. "Claudia ran out of the office, holding the Kemby, and headed for the other side of the building. I couldn't believe we didn't see anybody. Not a soul. She started treating the cubicles as a sort of maze, running in and out of the rooms. I tried, but I couldn't keep up with her."

"Reason enough to install doors," said Erica. "It might have slowed her down."

Dessie ignored this and went on. "I was glad that one office was open. Ron's. Thank God for his quirks. There was a box of those gloves on the desk. I grabbed a handful. One size fits all. I put one on each hand and the rest in my pants pocket. Then I went after her.

"By this time, she was heading down the stairs to the lobby, taunting me each step of the way," Dessie said. "She was chanting: 'The theater will close. They'll tear it down.'"

"'They'll pave paradise and put up a parking lot?'" Erica offered.

Dessie looked hard at her. "I don't think Claudia's repertoire included Joni Mitchell," she said.

"More of a Coldplay kind of girl?" Erica asked.

"More of a no-play kind of girl," said Dessie dismissively. "By then, she had gotten to the first floor and was heading down the corridor that separates the lobby from the ground-floor theater, where they were starting to set up for *Michelangelo*. It was pretty dark, and she tripped on a line of cable on the floor. It wasn't enough to upend her, just enough to slow her down. She stumbled and dropped the Kemby, and it fell into a pile of wires, which were coiled in the corner. I got there first, and grabbed it."

"With your gloves on," said Erica. "That leave no prints."

"Exactly," said Dessie. "Claudia's stumble slowed her down but didn't stop her. She was heading down the corridor, but what she didn't see was where it ended. It stops at a locked door. Behind the door is the closet where they keep the supplies for the concession stand. She didn't smash into the door—she wasn't moving that fast—but she did stop short. She just stopped. And she knew I was right behind her."

"But probably not expecting to get clocked with a Kemby," said Erica.

"Okay, yes, I hit her," Dessie admitted. "She wanted to destroy everything that has been built here. Anything that would be built in the future. I couldn't let that happen."

"Sorry to interrupt, but quick question, Dessie. Instead of getting the Kemby, why didn't you use that cute little revolver in your hand? If the theater was empty, no one would hear a shot—"

"The gun came later," Dessie said. "I told you, fresh off the prop table. And I borrowed it for your benefit, Erica," she finished. "Curious girl that you are, you ask a lot of questions."

"Dessie, really, you shouldn't have," said Erica. Wanting more than ever to keep the conversation going, she introduced a new topic of discussion.

"But staging the body, Dessie. Did you have to?"

"I could see she was hurt. And it was bad. I slipped off the first pair of gloves—they were *used*, shall we say—and I rolled them up, inside out, and put them in my other pocket. I took out a clean pair of gloves and put them on. I knew where the concessionaire keeps the key to the closet—it's in one of those hide-a-key things that attaches by magnet to the bottom of the metal display case—don't tell anyone, by the way. I don't want the supplies to disappear."

"Ever vigilant," said Erica.

"I got the key and opened the closet," Dessie continued. "The concessionaire keeps one of those rolling desk chairs in there, so he can sit during the down times between intermissions. With more than one theater running, audience members can appear at any moment, ready to buy merchandise. Anyway, I opened the door, got the chair out, and dragged Claudia onto it."

"I can personally attest to the fact that you're stronger than you look," said Erica, interrupting her.

"I'm a lot more things than I look," said Dessie, then continued, "It wasn't easy and I tried to keep her at arm's length as much as possible. No dropping hair and fibers for me. I've seen *CSI*. I know my forensics."

"And you were helped, no doubt, by the fact that the first-floor corridor is a virtual stampede of hair and fibers," said Erica.

"Techies do shed a lot," Dessie replied. "So do audience members," she added.

"So do the numberless people who walk in and out of this theater every day," Erica said. "But the staging, Dessie. Why?"

"Because, just because," answered Dessie. "Sometimes you have to improvise. What was I going to do? Lock her in the closet? Not many people know about the key, so that would limit the number of suspects. Besides, everything in the closet would be spoiled, contaminated by being near her. I couldn't let all those supplies go to waste. And I wasn't about to wheel her around the theater looking for a better hiding place. The place seemed empty, but you never know who you might meet. I looked around the corner, and I saw all the posters on display. Not the one for *Michelangelo: The Musical*. It was too soon. But the poster art had been approved, and we both know what it's going to look like.

"A rip-off of Michelangelo's *The Creation of Man*," said Erica.

"We prefer to think of it as an homage," Dessie countered. "I knew exactly where it was going to be displayed when the time came. So I put her there. Right underneath where the poster can be seen now. By the corner of the concession stand."

"Both hidden and revealed," said Erica. "Nice touch, Dessie. But if this is all about saving the theater, you didn't think that the small matter of a murder would be a problem? The supplies in the closet would not be the only things that were contaminated."

"Haven't you learned anything in this job, Erica?" asked Dessie. "There's no such thing as bad publicity.

And the poster for the show? We've already sold out the first run. People want it as a memento."

"Of the murder or the musical?" asked Erica.

"I don't know," Dessie answered. "You'd have to ask them."

Erica thought about this for a moment before moving to her next question.

"You sent me to Claudia's apartment, I assume with the intention of having me find Volume Two. You could have destroyed Claudia's journals, and the story would end there. 'A girl dies. How sad.' Why did you want me to find it?"

"Because of what I found. Yes, I did take race over to Claudia's apartment that night, and I did take a look around. With my trusty pair of gloves—I love those things. I can see why Ron is addicted to them. At the time, I didn't know that Volume One, as you call it, was still here in that permanent mess on top of her desk. When I checked her purse before I left the theater, I saw Volume Two, and I took it to look at later. I also got her keys and went straight to her apartment. I saw none of the neighbors, though I doubt anyone would have bothered with me. Claudia wasn't a people person, not even in her off hours. She was probably the phantom neighbor that no one ever saw. Maybe the building is full of phantom neighbors. Anyway, there was no one in the halls or on the stairs.

"And that apartment," Dessie continued. "I'd never been there before. I would never have let the kids go, under any circumstances. What a dump," she added with a dollop of Bette Davis. "Granted, it was a little neater before I got through with it, but it never looked like a home."

"Or even habitable," said Erica.

"Maybe so," said Dessie. "There was little enough to recommend it. And I didn't find much of anything.

With the exception of a file folder Claudia kept in her underwear drawer. Right under the Hanes Her Way. It was filled with treasures. It's where I found her birth certificate, the one listing the Winthrops as her parents. Oh, by the way, whatever happened to that note from her birth mother? I assume you have it, Erica."

Erica chose to give nothing away.

"Well, either you or the lady who cleans this office," Dessie shrugged. "Whatever. And then there was the grand prize, the big find. Claudia's original birth certificate, the one listing the names of her birth mother and dear old dad. Her father goes by the name of Unknown, in case you wondered. That's the one paper I had to have and couldn't let go of. That's what made it all worthwhile."

"Worthwhile?" said Erica. "Worth killing over?"

"Erica, let me be clear. That girl was not going destroy my chance to name a theater after Martin. She would be destroyed first."

Dessie was now on a roll, so she stood to play the scene for all it was worth with the gun still in play.

"I didn't know how soon the body would be discovered and the police would be on the scene. So I scooped up everything in the drawer, minus the undies, and I kept it until the all-clear was sounded. Then, with my gloves in hand, I would make a return trip to the apartment."

"Why did you put Volume Two back, leaving it for me to find?" Erica wanted to know.

"This was after the police had done their thing in Claudia's apartment, and after they returned her keys and belongings to me. God knows what that search told them. I thought you would find the journal, given where I hid it. That TV almost came down on me, so I figured it must fall on anyone who walked near it. By the looks of the place, I doubt Claudia had regular visitors, so maybe she had a way to keep it from toppling on her. Either you found the notebook, or the movers did, or no one did. Although you did hold onto it, which I didn't expect. I mean, you gave up Volume One right away."

"And I may have been willing to hand over Volume Two, if I hadn't found Volume One in the trash, thanks to a couple of dumpster divers."

"Well, now you have the complete set," said Dessie. "At least, I hope that's the complete set," she said, mostly to herself. "And you're a literary type, Erica. So enjoy." Dessie smiled as she continued. "It was strictly insurance. I wanted someone to know that Claudia had been adopted and that she was born in Maine, where, as I think we both know, with a copy of her birth certificate, the one listing the adoptive parents, plus a form and a fee, she could get her original birth certificate. Pretty simple. I'm sure the police could get that file unsealed if they wanted to. And there they'd see the name of her birth mother. The one who gave her away. Sold her? Who knows? The great and wonderful Alexa Wallace."

Dessie stopped for a moment.

"I can tell from your expression that none of this comes as a surprise to you," said Dessie. "You've been feeding me information all along. I knew what you wanted me to know when you wanted me to know it. But asking me to review the personnel files, Claudia's among them, that put you over the line. Funny that Claudia's is the only file that contains a birth certificate. The adoptive one, of course. I assume you kept the original."

"Well, that's as may be," Dessie said with another shrug. "Now, Alex didn't kill Claudia, and they would have a hard time proving she did, given her whereabouts. She was in a meeting with a few of the richest and most prominent people in New York. They tend to make good alibi witnesses. But it would take a while to work all of that out. And if Alex did get caught in the trap, who cares? Even she is expendable, if it comes to that."

"Everything in the service of the greater good," said Erica. "The greater good being the Martin McNulty Memorial Theater."

"It's something that his children can be proud of," Dessie insisted. "It will stand forever as a reminder of him and what he did with his life."

"It certainly could," said Erica. "But why would you try to pin the murder on Alex?" she asked.

"I know Alex is not guilty, and I know she can't be found guilty," Dessie said offhandedly, as if she were describing a matter of no consequence. "Some collateral damage to her reputation, maybe, but more than likely, no real harm, regardless of what crazy Claudia might think. And it could be fun to watch Alex talk her way out of this one. She would have an interesting time explaining who Mr. Unknown was. Then, the police would have to find him and sit him down for a talk. Did he do it? No. But that would take some time, time enough to finish my theater—I mean, Martin's theater—and after that, I honestly don't care."

"In whose honor is this theater being named, Dessie? Martin or you?" asked Erica.

"Martin, of course," Dessie answered, spitting out the words.

"Are you sure about that?" Erica insisted. "Is it a testament to his career, or to the one you might have had, if a bad heart hadn't changed your plans?"

"I could have had a career," Dessie began.

"Yes, Dessie, you could have been a contender. You'll get no argument here, and Alan would back me up on this. Based on the available evidence, you could have done what Martin never did, and have the career that you pretend he could have had. If a theater is named for him, then there's the undeniable proof that everything you want to believe about him, everything you want your children to believe, is true. The proof in steel and concrete that he was the man you wanted him to be. Even if he wasn't. Especially if he wasn't."

Dessie gave Erica a look that could politely be described as venomous, but said nothing. Erica continued.

"And yet, you seem almost as devoted to the People's Theater as you are to your family. You really didn't think the theater might suffer when a dead body was found in the lobby?"

Now this was a question Dessie could answer. Calmly, she replied, "I will say this one more time, Erica. Bad publicity. Good publicity. It's all the same. It's about exposure. You build it and they will come."

"And you already knew the truth about Claudia, didn't you, Dessie?"

"I had a pretty good idea when Claudia showed up with that pitiful story that she was up to something. Then I saw her birth date on the employment forms— month, day, and year. I'm so glad we ask for place of birth. And, as I said, I knew Alex back in the day. I was still acting and she already worked here. Part of the tee-shirt-and-jeans brigade. Starving actors, producer wannabes, theater groupies, what have you. Well, those tee shirts don't hide much. And one summer, twenty-odd years ago, maybe more like late spring, she started to put on weight. She took to wearing sweatshirts so no one would notice, but that wasn't going to fly as we got deeper into a New York summer. She asked for a leave of absence, made some vague excuse about a family matter—well, that couldn't be closer to the truth—and off she went, for her confinement, as they used to say in nineteenth-century plays."

"In which you have appeared," said Erica.

"Yes, but we'll save that for another day. As for Alex," Dessie said, "although we never discussed it, she knew that I knew. I never asked her who the baby-daddy was or why she hadn't, you know, used some kind of birth control. I mean, she was no teenager at the time. When she got pregnant, maybe even considered the alternative? But she hadn't, and she didn't, and it wasn't my business anyway. She left, went home to Maine, stayed for a few months, and then she came back. I was guessing at the time, but I knew for sure when she began taking the same day off each year, around the time in September when she would have given birth. Her one and only day off.

"I never knew what happened to the baby. I do know what happened to Alex. She came back alone and stayed that way. She was no field of flowers before she left, and after she came back, well, of course, she would be changed. Slowly but surely, she turned into the woman we know now—not without humanity, exactly, but steering clear of all the things that would make her human." Dessie paused for a moment. "I do miss the old girl, sometimes," she said wistfully.

She shrugged her shoulders as she turned her attention back to Erica.

"Well, that was a nice long speech," Dessie said. "I feel so much better now. And I know that you were trying to prolong the conversation until you figured out your next move, Erica. Or until the cavalry arrived." Dessie made the theatrical gesture of looking around the room. "But it's still just us girls," she said. "And I'd have to say that I was happy to indulge you because I'm not sure what my next move will be," Dessie admitted as she fondled the gun. "We'll just have to see."

"Be sure to keep me posted, Dessie," said Erica, taking a more aggressive approach now that subterfuge was a lost cause. "But let's be clear. I know you've been lying to me since Day One."

"What do you mean?" asked Dessie, slightly startled by this accusation.

"On the first day, at lunch, I asked you about Alex," Erica said.

"And I answered," replied Dessie.

"But not about Ally," Erica continued. "You left that part out. On that day and all the days that followed."

"Oh, you have done your research," said Dessie admiringly. "Well, let me be clear. You asked about Alex, and I told you. As much as is generally known."

"As much as I needed to know," replied Erica.

"Something like that," Dessie acknowledged. "Ally was a sweet girl I played basketball with a long time ago. Alex came into being sometime after that."

"You were friends, Dessie," Erica insisted. "You went through high school together."

"Took the team all the way to division finals one year. Go Spuds," said Dessie proudly, then abruptly returned to the present. "That was then. This is now. And now, we both play for the People's Theater. That's the one thing we share, the only thing we have in common," said Dessie firmly.

"But you also had Claudia in common," replied Erica. "And if she showed up with a see-through story, you couldn't let that go. You'd want to know for sure."

"Of course I did. And Claudia *did* leave that big bag of hers wide open in her desk drawer. Maybe she wanted to me look? In any case, her notebooks were there for the taking," said Dessie.

"And did you read her notebooks?" asked Erica.

"What do you think?" asked Dessie, daring her.

"I think it's a little late in the day to be probing Claudia's psychology," said Erica. "I don't think that will get us anywhere."

"That's a long story of its own," Dessie agreed. "Claudia was sent on many errands in her first few months here, to get a handle on the layout of the building. Mostly, she got lost. But I wanted her elsewhere to find out what I needed to know. Can you believe that she wouldn't have a driver's license? Where she's from, you can drive a tractor at the age of twelve. Luke would move there in a minute," said Dessie, smiling as she mentioned her son. "That may be an exaggeration, and Claudia may have had a license, but I couldn't find it."

"How inconvenient for you," said Erica.

"It was, at first," nodded Dessie. "I thought the license would be the first step in finding out who she really was."

"And you had to kill her to get her birth certificate?" asked Erica.

"No, I had to kill her to stop her from ruining my plans. The birth certificate, that was just a bonus," said Dessie brightly.

"Did her high school diploma happen to be in her bag?" Erica wanted to know.

"What?" asked Dessie, surprised by the question.

"I was just wondering," said Erica. "If her birth mother was a local girl, and the adoption seems to have taken place in the general vicinity, maybe Claudia grew up riding her bicycle on the same streets, drinking the same water, and going to the same schools as her birth mother did. Maybe she walked the halls of the same high school, admiring the trophies, maybe even looking at the pictures, of the women who would turn out to be her mother . . . and her murderer. Which high school did Claudia go to?" asked Erica.

"I don't remember," said Dessie, determined to forget.

"I wished I shared the same amnesia," said Erica. "Go Spuds."

Dessie, for the first time, looked uncertain.

"And while we're at it, there must be more than one Alexa Wallace in the phone book," continued Erica. "I wonder how Claudia knew exactly where to look. I mean, she did land on the doorstep of the People's Theater. 'Kerplunk,' as they say, but there she was."

Dessie had resumed her pose of calm as she waved the gun for emphasis. "That's as may be," she said. "As you said, a little late in the day to debate it. Still, you know, it's nice to be able to share my story with someone who can fully appreciate it, but can say nothing."

"And why not?" asked Erica.

"Oh, go ahead, sing out, Louise. It would be your word against mine. And I will be the one denying it."

"Why do you think that you would be believed—whatever you said?" asked Erica.

"Let's see," said Dessie. "My word—spoken by a hard-working, single mother of two. A friend to the deceased, who even invited the poor girl into her home and trusted her with her children. And then there's you. Someone died at the last place you worked, didn't they? Of course, you had nothing to do with it, but it is an odd coincidence. What with you in the general vicinity of another person who died under, shall we say, unusual circumstances."

"So, you knew before you hired me," said Erica.

"Actually, I didn't," said Dessie. "I only knew what Alan and your resume told me. But we don't all have to take long walks to the library to find out what we need to know. Some of us are content to sit at our desks and let the internet do the walking. A quick search, and I had all the information I needed."

"Was this a little more insurance?" Erica asked.

"Just in case I needed it," Dessie said. She smiled. "You don't seem to get it, Erica. I had to kill Claudia. No one and nothing was going to get between me and the theater with Martin's name on it. *No one*."

Erica quickly understood that Dessie included her in that number. Still, she chose to persist, saying, "Someone has gotten in the way of that. You."

"I don't think so," Dessie replied. "Why would it? And if it should come down to a case of she said/she said, I'll win hands down. Given a choice, who would you believe?"

Before Erica could reply, someone stepped out of the shadows and answered for her.

"Would they believe me, Dessie?" Alex asked.

How long she had been standing in the darkened outer office was anybody's guess. But Alex had heard enough.

At the sound of Alex's voice, Dessie dropped the gun but made no attempt to retrieve it. Luckily, the gun made a soft landing on the carpet and skittered to the other side of the room, out of harm's way. Even with her ability to hold center stage, Dessie could barely get out the words "What are you doing here?"

"I came back for something I left in the office," Alex said, seemingly unfazed by the sight of Dessie, Erica, or the gun. "It was the budget for the new theater upstairs. The theater without a name. What luck I popped in when I did, don't you think? And how are you, Erica?" she finished, as if glad-handing at a fundraising event.

"So, Dessie, do you think I would be reliable enough as a witness?" Alex continued. "I can tell them everything. What I just heard, what the truth is, and even more importantly, the identity of Claudia's father, you know, the baby-daddy?"

Alex stopped for a moment and shook her head. "I had no idea who Claudia was. I passed her every day and felt nothing. No maternal pangs, I promise you. But you may feel one, Dessie. Because you obviously have no idea of the damage you've done. To this girl, to your own children, even to Martin's memory. Yes, Martin, I knew him. So many women did. That was no secret. All before he met you. But the part you didn't know, that even he didn't know, was that he got at least one of them pregnant. She never told him about the pregnancy. She did not see a future with him after a drunken one-night stand that was a bad idea from the start. But she did have the baby. Gave it up for adoption. To a nice family with a good home."

Dessie seemed to be using every inch of her five-foot frame to will Alex not to continue.

"Dessie, you killed Martin's child."

It was as if a switch had been flicked. Dessie, who looked stricken from the moment of Alex's arrival, now withdrew into herself. Instead of an outward show of anger, or possibly remorse, she wrapped her arms tightly around herself and began to moan, rocking forward, like the keening women in Irish plays. This continued as Alex, always the professional, hastily called the authorities after first taking the gun into her own custody, then alerted Dessie's baby sitter, who would be in for a long night. Both gun and bullets were later ascertained to be quite real—no faking it for Dessie—unless the onset of catatonia was a hoax. Dessie did not let up when the police arrived and took a statement from Alex and one from Erica. Dessie's statement consisted of more moaning, interrupted by the occasional sigh. Whether her trance was genuine or self-induced, it was convincing. Dessie was immediately transported to the nearest mental facility for observation.

CHAPTER 26

"Scratch an actor, and underneath you will find another actor."
Sir Laurence Olivier

"And there she sits," said Erica to Alan, who had returned from his adventure in Prague, bearing gifts that would make a Times Square schlock merchant blush.

"And Dessie's asked to see you?" said Alan. "I'm surprised she wants you anywhere near her."

"I'm surprised she's coherent enough to make requests. Last time I saw her, she was not quite at the point of catatonia, but hovering in the vicinity."

"Yes, we should talk about that night sometime," said Alan.

"I told you what happened," Erica quickly answered.

"I'm thinking more of what led up to it," he said. "And all the bits you left out."

"Another time," Erica said. "I promise."

"Just one thing for now," he said. "How much damage could Claudia really have done, waving around her birth certificate? Alex may have given her up, but she didn't leave her on the sidewalk."

"I think logic had very little to do with it, for Claudia or for Dessie," Erica replied. "According to her notebooks, Claudia was enraged by the fact that she had not been just given away, but that money apparently changed hands, and that it paid Alex's way back to the life she really wanted, and away from the daughter she really didn't. Claudia was 'sold,' as she put it. And

Claudia was certain that the world would share her outrage."

"Either she doesn't get out a lot, or she knows nothing about the theater," said Alan.

"Both, I would say," Erica offered. "I don't think we're talking about anything criminal on Alex's part. She seemed to be making the best of an unplanned pregnancy that she saw through to the end, and no further. But Claudia was convinced that even a whiff of scandal—and the hint of a profit motive—would bring the world Alex had made for herself tumbling down. Whether Claudia was right or wrong in gauging public opinion, *she* believed it, and that was all that mattered to her."

"She was deluded," said Alan.

"So was Dessie," Erica added. "Dessie was working on the theory that any glitch in the process would end her dream of a theater named after Martin—so she did what she felt she had to. That dream would come true, or else."

"And when their delusions crossed paths . . ." Alan said.

"Catastrophe," Erica finished. "But not the catastrophe either one was expecting."

"And Martin was the daddy," said Alan.

"Apparently," Erica replied.

"I guess I should have seen that one coming," Alan began, "but I never would have put Alex and Martin together."

"It was a one-off," said Erica. "Never to be repeated. In word or in deed."

She took a breath. "Is that enough for now?" she asked.

"Yes," said Alan. "You still haven't told me everything you knew, and when you knew it. But I know you will, eventually."

"Understood," Erica promised, before reverting to the previous subject. "Anyway, Alex is the one who's probably not on the visitor's list," she said. "But Dessie may have something more she wants to share. Would you care to join me?"

"Thank you, no. She asked for you, not me. This one is all yours," said Alan.

Erica had no idea why Dessie wanted to see her. Should she expect anger, an apology, or a request for magazines to while away the hours? Upon her arrival at the facility where Dessie currently resided, she was told that Dessie was allowed one visitor at a time, and only under supervision. If Alan had chosen to accompany her, he would have been left in the lobby.

Actions spoke louder than words in the halls of this facility. A young male attendant would observe the visit from behind a Plexiglas window so thick that you would have to stand right next to it and scream if you wanted to be heard. The attendant would be able to see everything, and was ready to spring into action if the conversation got too lively. Erica was also informed that the room was not miked or otherwise monitored to respect the patient's privacy. "Kind of like a prison visit," she had said in reply. No one was amused.

Given her appearance as she entered the room, any sudden movement on Dessie's part seemed unlikely. Dessie looked as if she'd lost about a foot in height and gained at least a decade in years. Dressed in a standard-issue hospital robe, covering a standard-issue hospital shirt, which on Dessie doubled as a nightgown, she shuffled in on a pair of slippers at least two sizes too large. With a matronly nurse at her side, Dessie was seated at a metal table in a chair diagonally opposite Erica, so that the attendant could see the patient's face and watch her actions and reactions. The chair could be moved, which Erica found odd, given that this would be much easier for an agitated patient to hurl than the table that had been bolted to the floor. Once the nurse left the room, the visitor was on her own. Seated across from Dessie, Erica was free to say whatever she wanted, as long as Dessie sat quietly and listened.

At first it seemed that Dessie was not even up to listening. She gazed in her visitor's direction but focused on Erica's right ear instead of her face. Erica let this go until she remembered who had called the meeting. Assuming Dessie hadn't mimed the request, Erica was certain that there was something more that needed to be said. She decided to blink first.

Placing her face unavoidably in Dessie's range of vision, Erica repeated her listener's name several times, each time more forcefully. "Dessie," Erica insisted, "I know you asked to see me. I think you have something you want to tell me. So I'll talk, at least until you're ready."

Dessie looked at Erica and made fleeting eye contact. Then, the patient turned her head to stare at the cinderblock wall. Erica was undaunted. This one-sided conversation would continue until Dessie decided to join it.

"How are they treating you, Dessie?"

No answer.

"Do you get enough to eat?"

Still no answer.

"Are you sleeping?" Erica asked.

No answers were forthcoming. The wall had all of Dessie's attention.

"Are you taking any interesting medications?"

This question answered itself. From the look of things, Dessie had ingested everything in the pharmacy.

"Have you been able to see your children?"

This struck a chord, as Erica knew it would.

"No, no, no, no, no!" said Dessie, pounding the table with clenched fists each time she said the word. Dessie's outburst got the attendant's attention, and he was immediately in the room, standing at her side.

Dessie calmly looked up at him, striking a penitent pose.

"Dessie, you're going to be a good girl or you're going back to your room. Do you understand me?" he asked in a firm but still friendly manner.

The patient breathed a small "yes." The attendant was placated and resumed his position behind the window.

Watching Dessie return to a state of calm, Erica was reminded how, in ancient Greece, the Furies, the goddesses of vengeance, drove people mad by turning up the volume on their interior monologue, on the things they would rather not remember. She wondered if this was driving Dessie, and if Dessie could turn down the volume on the narrative only Dessie could hear.

Erica also wondered at the rapid-fire change in Dessie's emotions. In a few minutes, the patient had gone from catatonic to enraged to chastened. No shifting of gears, no modulation, just a full-on rush from one to the next. If this were an acting class, it would be an impressive display, as if she were trying out every feeling at her disposal until she found the right one. Suddenly, Erica knew which emotion Dessie was searching for. The one that would get her where she wanted to go: Home. Home, by way of a verdict of not guilty. Not guilty by reason of mental disease or defect. A killer, yes, but not responsible for her actions. Still crazy but not culpable.

As defense strategies go, it was a huge gamble on Dessie's part, though no more of a risk than killing Claudia and then hiding her body in plain sight. Once

Dessie had been found out, and facing a certain conviction, her last resort, the only thing over which she still had control, was her acting ability. Maybe this was the plan all along. Their meeting was an audition, Erica realized, not intended for Alan or another actor, but for a non-actor, a civilian, who make up most of the jury pool. Erica was also convinced that Dessie needed her to see this: if the stars had aligned a little differently, Dessie truly could have achieved the success that she had fabricated for Martin.

Watching Dessie go through her paces, Erica was reminded of when Alan was preparing to play Iago. He had to find a reason for everything the character did, and accept it as his own. Whether Iago destroyed lives because he lacked advancement or because he had a big fat crush on Othello—whatever motivation made sense to the character had to make sense to the actor playing him. In the same way that Alan convincingly brought into being Iago's reasons for destroying a good man and his equally good woman, Dessie had to find her own logic unassailable. It was all plausible to her, including the part where she could avoid punishment for an action that she would not see as wrong. Maybe she was crazy after all.

"Dessie, I'm beginning to understand why I'm here," said Erica in an audible whisper. This got Dessie's attention, and she finally looked at Erica. At the same time, Dessie began to rock back and forth in her seat, showing some agitation, but not enough to earn a return visit from the attendant.

"You're confusing symptoms," said Erica. "The rocking is more autism than insanity. You don't want to veer into *Rain Man* territory."

Erica had Dessie's full attention now. The eyes that had looked blankly, then angrily, then calmly in Erica's direction, now reverted to a gaze she recognized as

Dessie's own, a look that was unfiltered and lacking in disguise. Unlike the staff, who treated this patient like a fragile piece of glass, Erica knew Dessie was made of sterner stuff. She doubted that Dessie would go in for head banging, but before the patient decided to expand her symptoms to cowering like a calf, or worse, started to moo, Erica needed to make the most of this lucid moment.

"I suggest you stick with psychosis, Dessie, but maybe dial it back a bit. You've got quite a range, but you don't want to hit them with everything at once. Less is usually more."

Dessie stared wide eyed but still said nothing.

"I'm just saying, pick a lane, or at least, a progression," Erica instructed. "Don't start by ricocheting off the walls. It's too hard to sustain. Build to a climax. Just like in a play."

"Keep it fresh as they say," Erica continued. "As if it's happening for the first time. As if you don't know how the story ends."

Erica met Dessie in a level gaze, which Dessie returned.

"And don't forget to play it as if your life depended on it," Erica finished.

"It's too bad you never saw me act," Dessie said quietly, as herself.

"Oh, but I have," Erica replied.

Their time was up, as the nurse's return made clear, and Dessie was lifted from her seat and assisted out of the room. She seemed to be sticking with the enfeebled Dessie for the time being, too incapacitated to hurt a fly or be tried for murder. As Dessie left the room, Erica heard her softly humming the overture to *The Brothers Wittgenstein.*

The mad scene, thought Erica. *Exit Ophelia.*

CHAPTER 27

"I want to do everything in the world that can be done."
Fanny Kemble

"As psychotic breaks go, I'd have to say that this one seemed a little rehearsed," said Erica to Alan, as she finished describing what she'd seen during her visit. "I don't know if Dessie has an analyst or an acting coach working with her, but she's giving it her all."

"What is *it*?" Alan wanted to know.

"*It* is a verdict of 'not guilty by reason of mental disease,'" answered Erica. "Well, let me back up a little. I'd say she's prepping for a 7:30 exam, the one where she can be deemed incompetent to stand trial. That's based on her competence at the time of the trial. Failing that, her back up would seem to be an insanity defense—which would reflect her state of mind at the time of the crime—with a resounding NOT GUILTY at the end of it. Oh, it's *non compos mentis* all the way for our Dessie."

"She told you all this?" asked Alan.

"She told me nothing," said Erica. "I watched and learned."

"You're sure she's acting?"

"Asked the actor," Erica replied.

"Do you think Dessie will get away with it?"

"Alan, if that's an act, then she's still got it," Erica said. "It's not a Kemby-winning performance yet. Still in previews. She's trying out different forms of crazy, dialing it up and down. But with enough rehearsal, who knows?"

"You saw through her," said Alan. "Why wouldn't a jury?"

"Because I know her," said Erica. "I have observed her at close range, both sane and crazy. I must say, her crazy is pretty impressive. But I'm not really equipped to judge her competency or her acting ability. I'll leave that to the experts."

"Still, it's a pretty tall order," said Alan.

"Well, the staff at the facility seems to be buying it, and they must have seen a few fakes in their time," replied Erica. "My money's on Dessie. The sentimental favorite."

"And stone-cold killer," said Alan. "Speaking of your friends at the People's Theater, someone named Monty called—"

"Are you sure?" Erica interjected.

"Quite sure," said Alan, a little testy. "She identified herself as Alex's new assistant."

"Welcome back, Monty," Erica said. "That must have been an interesting conversation. Well, I guess if your old friend betrays you, you may as well go with a clean slate."

"Not that clean," said Alan.

"Oh, the small matter of being fired without cause," said Erica. "Bygones. And I'm sure Alex offered her a sweet deal."

"No doubt, we'll all be working for Monty one day," said Alan. "Anyway, Monty said that due to budget cutbacks, your position has been—what word did she use?—oh, that's right, *suspended*."

"Am I supposed to show up in detention?" asked Erica.

"I think she means you've been fired," Alan said.

"Well, if Monty's working there, they're going on a last-fired, first-hired basis. So they should be calling me any day now," Erica ventured.

"Don't hold your breath," Alan replied. "I'd say it was a good thing you cleaned out your desk the last time you were there. You didn't leave anything behind?"

"Just a little piece of my heart," said Erica.

"Well," said Alan, "those tend to grow back."

"I assume Alex is bearing up," Erica began.

"Monty didn't say," answered Alan. "And I didn't ask."

"Did Monty say anything about the much-anticipated production of *Michelangelo: The Musical*?"

"No, but I think the show will go on, as if there were any doubt," said Alan. "They have Miranda out flogging the production, acting up a storm in television interviews. She swears that returning to the theater is all she has dreamed of—"

"Since she left?" finished Erica. "Well, it's nice for Kenny, anyway. His big break. And for Alex, I guess. I imagine she's diving back into her work."

"I would think so," Alan said. "That seems to be her comfort zone."

"At least she isn't playing the grieving mother," said Erica.

"Since she barely knew her daughter, I'd say that's a role that should be underplayed," said Alan, brushing aside the suggestion. "And your future with the People's Theater seems to be limited to their offer of two tickets for opening night at *Michelangelo*. It should be a star-studded affair."

"Will you be there?" asked Erica.

"Wouldn't miss it," he said. "Plus, they're sending over a copy of the poster. A big thank you for all you did—"

"In finding the person who killed Claudia?"

"They didn't put it quite that way," said Alan. "Another role that's being underplayed."

"Funny way to say you're fired," said Erica. "And what about Dessie's theater?"

"Monty didn't mention it," Alan replied. "But the news on the Rialto is that they're selling the naming rights."

"That's the American way," Erica said. "Want to put in a bid?"

"I think we're a few million short," said Alan. "And what would we call it?"

"Don't ask," said Erica. "But when you think about it, Claudia did destroy what Dessie held most dear— and it was not the chance to name a theater after Martin. It was the mythology surrounding him, created and nurtured by Dessie."

"Are you sure about that?" asked Alan. "In a way, I hope it's still keeping Dessie warm at night."

"Maybe," said Erica. "But her ignorance about Martin, willed or not, was what made the rest of her life possible."

Erica was fairly certain that Dessie currently dreamed of a speedy competency hearing, followed by a not-guilty verdict, and a speedier recovery. Then, having been found not a danger to herself or others, it would be home to her children, who, Erica had heard, were living with an aunt and uncle in Maine. If they had to make the sudden switch from city kids to country cousins, Erica hoped that Luke was riding high on a tractor.

"What are you thinking about?" asked Alan, who noticed.

"Nothing much," said Erica, "other than the fact that there's been a whole lot of acting going on. Not just Dessie. Claudia put on her own little show. I wonder how incompetent she really was. Or if she inherited some acting ability from Martin. Which makes me think he was a better actor than he got credit for."

"He had his moments," said Alan.

"Dessie seemed to think so," said Erica.

"Yes," said Alan, "and she killed to prove the point."

"Maybe the point couldn't have been proven, at least to her, in any other way," Erica said.

"Then she really is crazy," Alan replied.

"Trust me, she's not," said Erica. "Okay, maybe I can't judge Dessie's state of mind now as she does her seven performances a week for an audience of healthcare professionals. But everything leading up to this finale was a well-conceived plan, and that includes lying to me on a daily basis. Maybe not lies of commission—not all of them, anyway—but lies of omission, definitely. There was a whole lot she left out."

"Yes, those lies of omission can get you every time," said Alan.

"Okay," Erica admitted. "I'm not saying that Dessie is the only one guilty of that particular offense."

"I thought this was the one you were going to let go," said Alan.

"It was," said Erica. "And I did."

Alan looked skeptical.

"Okay, I did at first. Then I followed Dessie's lead, and lead me she did, from beginning to end. Putting the pieces together with her expert, usually unseen, help."

"We can decide your punishment later," Alan said, almost serious. "But either way, whether she is found guilty or not responsible for her actions, what Dessie did had an awful cost. For Dessie, for her children, for Alex—"

"For Martin's child," Erica added.

"For everyone connected to this," Alan finished.

"I think that a nice hot shower will take care of me," said Erica.

"I'd like to think so, too," said Alan, sounding less convinced. "So what's next on your agenda? After the shower, I mean."

"I don't have an agenda," Erica replied. "And I don't have a next. There's only one thing I'm reasonably sure about," she said.

"What's that?" Alan asked, expectantly.

"Well," said Erica, "that's show biz."

THE END

ABOUT THE AUTHOR

Laura Shea is a professor of English at Iona College in New Rochelle, New York. She is the author of *A Moon for the Misbegotten on the American Stage*, and her essays and reviews have appeared in *The Eugene O'Neill Review*, *Theatre Journal*, *Theatre Annual*, *The Comparatist*, and *American Theater Web*. She has also worked in different professional capacities in theaters in Boston and New York. In addition to *Murder at the People's Theater*, she is also the author of *A Dying Fall*, a mystery novel set in academe. She lives in New York City.

www.ingramcontent.com/pod-product-compliance
Lightning Source LLC
Chambersburg PA
CBHW020327260626
47156CB00004B/1415